# Grateful for the Sheikh

*A Novel by*

# Annabelle Winters

# Books by Annabelle Winters

## The CURVES FOR SHEIKHS Series

*Curves for the Sheikh*
*Flames for the Sheikh*
*Hostage for the Sheikh*
*Single for the Sheikh*
*Stockings for the Sheikh*
*Untouched for the Sheikh*
*Surrogate for the Sheikh*
*Stars for the Sheikh*
*Shelter for the Sheikh*
*Shared for the Sheikh*
*Assassin for the Sheikh*
*Privilege for the Sheikh*
*Ransomed for the Sheikh*
*Uncorked for the Sheikh*
*Haunted for the Sheikh*
*Grateful for the Sheikh*
*Mistletoe for the Sheikh*
*Fake for the Sheikh*

# GRATEFUL FOR THE SHEIKH

## A NOVEL BY

# ANNABELLE WINTERS

2018
RAINSHINE BOOKS
USA

# Copyright Notice

Copyright © 2018 by Annabelle Winters
All Rights Reserved by Author
www.annabellewinters.com
ab@annabellewinters.com

If you'd like to copy, reproduce, sell, or distribute any part of this text, please obtain the explicit, written permission of the author first. Note that you should feel free to tell your spouse, lovers, friends, and coworkers how happy this book made you. Have a wonderful evening!

Cover Design by S. Lee

ISBN:  9781790219247

0 1 2 3 4 5 6 7 8 9

# Grateful for the Sheikh

**1**

Penelope Peterson filled in the small grave beside the grove of birch trees. This wasn't a sad occasion. Although she cried each time one of her birds died, her heart was always full because it reminded her of what she was doing and why she was doing it.

"You run a turkey farm, but you don't kill or sell the turkeys. You know that's insane, don't you? I mean, I get that you're a vegetarian nutcase, but come on, Pen. How do you earn a living?"

Pen had taken a breath and stared at her friend Willow, the Goth-styled, heavily tattooed waif of a woman who was almost forty but looked like she was twenty-five. Pen herself was closer to twenty-five than forty, but she looked . . . well, Pen just liked to say she spent a lot of time in the sun. With her birds. And her plants. And her . . . eggs.

"Turkey eggs. They're a thing, you know," Pen would reply to anyone who questioned her decision to take over her parents' turkey farm and then decide to stop slaughtering the danged turkeys! "They're gonna catch on. I just know it."

"The powerful chicken lobby will shut you down before turkey-egg omelets ever catch on," Willow had declared the last time they'd talked about it—which was just over a month earlier, when the electric company had turned off the power after sixty days of nonpayment and Willow and Pen had sat on the porch under the North Dakota stars and sipped stove-top brewed tea while pondering the universe and its mysteries.

"Well, I've also been thinking about what I can do with the turkey feathers," Pen said excitedly as she sniffed her chamomile tea and made a face. "Does this tea smell weird to you?"

"The only thing that smells weird is your head, because I think your brain is rotting away inside it," Willow firmly declared, checking her black nailpolish and sighing. "You need to come up with a plan, Pen." She paused, raising a carefully plucked, jet-black eyebrow. "You also need to come up with a man. How long has it been since David?"

"David who?" said Pen, putting down her cup and crossing one leg over the other. She hated talking about David, but Willow insisted on bringing up the topic. David, who'd showed up with a fake diamond ring and a marriage proposal that was about as half-hearted as everything David did. David, who'd moved in with her and then decided he wanted to push back the wedding date a couple of years.

"We're engaged, so what's the rush to get married?" he'd told her. "I've got a lot going on at work, and I don't want to be distracted."

"You work at the post office in Fargo, and you haven't been promoted in almost five years," Pen had reminded him, her tone judgmental in a way that surprised her. She'd never grudged David the choices he'd made: dropping out of high school, running with the wrong crowd for far too long, and then sobering up to find out that he was thirty-two and worked at the post-office—and not as a mailman. He was still working a job where his peers were high-school kids taking a summer off before college. The realization had pissed him off, and it seemed like instead of trying to better himself he dealt with it the way he handled everything: By first ignoring it, then postponing it, and finally directing his frustration outwards.

"You ever thought about doing your hair and nails real nice for a change?" he'd asked one evening when Pen had returned from burying one of her birds, her fingernails brown with dirt, her hair tied back in a ragged ponytail.

"You ever thought about finishing high school?" she'd shot back, knowing it was rude but feeling short on patience with her sulky fiancé.

"Whoa," he'd said, turning his head from where he was laying on the couch, beer balanced on his soft gut. "How did this become about me?"

"How did *what* become about you?" Pen had answered, smiling sweetly and undoing her ponytail so her dark brown tresses hung down over her neck and shoulders. "Is this a thing? Are we fighting? Or are you just sitting on the couch, drinking a beer, and asking me why my hair and nails aren't perfect when I've been out working in the fields."

"You mean burying one of those old turkeys. That's not work. That's the opposite of work, if anything. Hell, each one of those birds is worth cold, hard cash, Penny."

"Don't call me Penny," Pen had said. "My mom called me Pen, and I like Pen."

He'd ignored her, like he always did when she asked him not to call her Penny. "At least your mom had the sense to know she was running a turkey farm, and turkeys are raised to be slaughtered and eaten."

"Mom is gone, and the farm is mine. I'm changing how we do things around here, and you know that. I'm gonna turn this into a different sort of farm. A place of warmth and compassion. And let me tell you, it took something out of Mom every time Thanksgiving came around and she knew her birds were going to end up on dinner tables all over the state. She did it because that's what Dad left her when he died, and she did it to put me through college so I *wouldn't* have to do it."

"They're dumb birds, Penny. Birds that are worth money. They ain't worth shit if you wait until they die natural deaths and then bury them like they's people."

"Like they *are* people," Pen said, knowing David hated it when she corrected his grammar. "*They's* is not a word."

"There you go condescending me again," he'd said. But he hadn't gotten angry. David didn't get angry. He got sad and sulky, and he hunched his shoulders and moped about the house in a way that made Pen *want* to "condescend him," whatever the hell that meant.

But Pen kinda knew what that meant, and she knew she was doing it. She hated herself for it sometimes, and she wished she could just tell him the truth: That maybe he needed to get off his ass and improve himself. Not for her, necessarily—she'd already agreed to accept him the way he was—but for *himself*! She hadn't really thought through a lot of it until he'd asked to marry her and then promptly given up his apartment and moved into the farmhouse with her.

And things had started to go downhill pretty quickly when she realized that spending all day, every day with this man was going to take something out of her . . . something she didn't want to give up.

She didn't know what it was—or perhaps she didn't want to admit what it was. Self respect? Not really, she'd thought. Although David had a tendency to get passive-aggressive, he wasn't disrespectful as such. So what was it, she'd wondered? What was it that made her heart almost leap with joy after he'd casually suggested that they push back the wedding and just stay engaged for another year or two.

"So are we calling off the engagement?" she'd asked him, not sure why she was actually relieved as she glanced at the fake diamond on her finger.

"No!" he'd said hurriedly, and when she saw the panicked way in which he'd glanced around her living room from his fixed spot on the couch, Pen knew he was more worried about losing his rent-free residence than her big round ass. "I just want to focus on work for now. You know how it is, babe."

"I know how what is? Focusing on work? Sure. I've been working since I was five. Do *you* know what focusing on work means?"

"What're you saying?" he'd snapped, finally swinging his legs off the couch, letting out a burp as he did it.

"I'm saying you call in sick once a month to work.

You show up late at least once a week. You don't read. You don't take classes. You've shown no interest in even finishing high-school, let alone anything else."

David had shaken his head and rubbed his eyes. Then he'd burped again. "All right, Penny. Forget I said anything. We'll get married this year, all right? Forget I said anything. Jeez!"

How fucking romantic, Pen had thought, turning from him so he wouldn't see the way she tightened her jaw. And in that moment she'd understood that feeling, that hesitation, that moment of relief mixed with sheer joy when she'd realized she had a way out: It was the feeling that she was settling, giving herself to a man way below her standards. There was nothing "wrong" with David as such. He was like a hundred other guys she'd gone to high-school with in Fargo—mostly decent, but without ambition or drive, happy to settle for a life of complacency, beer, and television. Nothing wrong with relaxing with a drink and a good show or the ballgame, but it couldn't be the only thing that motivated you in life. Nope. She wanted more.

And she wanted a man who wanted more.

The only question that bothered her after she'd shaken her head and given David his fake diamond ring back (along with two weeks to move out of her farmhouse . . .) was did she *deserve* a man who wanted more?

## 2

"Ya Allah! What have I done to deserve this?"

Sheikh Rafeez Al-Zahaar stared through the window of his private jet as the silver airplane broke through the cloud cover. He could still barely see through the snowflakes plastered on the double-paned windows, but as the plane began its descent he was able to discern the outline of the city of Fargo, North Dakota. It did not look like much, and the Sheikh grunted and glanced at his diamond-studded Patek-Phillipe watch.

"Five in the evening and already it is dark as night," he said out loud, shaking his head and sighing as he wondered how long he would actually have to stay in the American Midwest. He'd agreed to attend a college friend's wedding in Fargo, but already the Sheikh was regretting saying yes. He hated the cold. He hated the snow. And he hated it when the sun set at five in the goddamn evening!

"I can't believe you're actually coming, Raf!" Charlotte Goodwin had gushed over the phone when the Sheikh had finally taken her call after she'd tried to reach him incessantly.

I cannot believe it either, Rafeez had thought as he fought the feeling that this was a bad idea. Why was Charlotte inviting him to her damned wedding? He'd banged her a few times when they'd met at Oxford a decade earlier. She was a Rhodes Scholar from America, and they'd only overlapped a few months before the Sheikh took his degree and went back to rule his kingdom of Zahaar. That had always been the plan, and he'd never lied to Charlotte about what they were doing. She'd understood—indeed she seemed almost happy with their arrangement at the time. And that was just fine with Rafeez. He'd never really connected with her, and the sex was no better or worse than what he was getting from a dozen other women who walked the fabled halls of Oxford University. In fact he'd forgotten about Charlotte until she'd sent him an invitation to her wedding and then called about a hundred times to beg him to attend.

"I'm Associate Professor of Middle Eastern Studies at the University of North Dakota," she'd explained when the Sheikh made it clear from his tone that he almost certainly was not going to fly across the world to attend the wedding of some minor fling whose name he could barely remember. "I'm up for tenure this year, and it would look really great if you showed up at the wedding."

"Because I am the only Arab you know?" he'd asked, raising an eyebrow as he sighed and glanced at his calendar for November of that year. Strangely enough, he was scheduled to be in New York City at the end of the month for a meeting with his American investment advisors. And he did not have any major commitments in Zahaar the week before, which was when Charlotte's wedding was scheduled.

"Oh, I know *lots* of Arabs," Charlotte had said, her tone somehow angering the Sheikh. "But you're the only Arab *king* in my life."

"I prefer the title Sheikh," Rafeez had said coldly, glancing at his calendar again. He still had that sinking feeling in his gut that this was a bad idea. From what he remembered of her, Charlotte was brilliant and ambitious—both good things—but also prone to justifying behavior that the Sheikh considered borderline unethical. "And I am *not* in your life, Charlotte."

But in the end the Sheikh had agreed—not because Charlotte was particularly convincing or that he particularly wanted to see her, but because he decided it made sense from a perception standpoint. Or at least

*Grateful for the Sheikh*

it might in the future. After all, Charlotte was an eloquent speaker, and her height and looks projected a convincing image when she took the stage. Who knew where she would be in five years, ten years, fifteen years? She had picked Middle Eastern Studies as her academic career, and if the Sheikh knew anything about Charlotte, he knew it was all calculated. Being recognized as a Middle East expert would get you lucrative advisory and consultancy gigs with corporations as well as the U.S. government. In either case, it would be good business and good politics to maintain cordial relations with Charlotte. Do her a favor by gracing her wedding with your royal presence. Make her look like a Middle East expert in front of her colleagues and friends. Then she will owe you favors for years to come. American corporations setting up branches in the kingdom of Zahaar based on Charlotte's advice? And it never hurts to have an insider who owes you favors when it comes to the U.S. government, yes?

Yes, the Sheikh had said, but now as he gritted his teeth as his jet skidded to a stop on the small runway of Fargo's airport, the snow falling like cannonballs from an ashen sky, he wondered if he should have said no. Perhaps he should never have taken the woman's call. By Allah, he should have his head examined for even being here! Five days in what appeared to be the goddamn Arctic Circle!

The wedding itself was a surprisingly modest affair,

and the Sheikh did his bit by playing the Arabian king. He wore a tailored black tuxedo and a forty-thousand dollar Rolex with diamonds that shone brighter than the bride's wedding ring. He showed off his perfect white teeth and manicured jawline-stubble, demonstrated his firm handshake, made up stories of camel-races and being lost in sand-storms.

By the end of it he was somewhat on edge, though, and when he finally took a break from entertaining the other guests, a strange feeling of disgust washed over him. Disgust at himself. What in Allah's name was he doing here? Was this what his life had come to? Playing a stereotype for the amusement of Americans just so he could buy himself some favors from a woman who might someday be in a position to grant them? What had happened to his ambitions of putting Zahaar on the world map? Raising its profile in the eyes of the world? Was he not thinking big enough? Trying hard enough?

Patience, he told himself. These things take time. Sometimes you have to let things develop at their own pace. It is fine to want more and to want it now, but one must make sure to always—

"May I get you a drink, sir?" came the interruption, and the Sheikh glanced up at the petite, dark-haired waif of a woman who looked like a boy with her short hair and flat chest. She was clearly one of the caterers, and the Sheikh raised an eyebrow and tapped his knuckles on the empty glass.

"Club soda. One slice of lemon."

"Ice?" she asked.

The Sheikh gestured with his head towards the window across from them. "Who takes ice in the middle of an ice-storm?" he grunted. He looked at her name tag and glanced up into her eyes. She was older than she looked from a distance, and the Sheikh did not find her attractive. He suspected the feeling was mutual, and it occurred to him that this woman was not into men at all. Perfect. "Are you from the area, Miss Willow?" he asked, glancing at her name tag once more to make sure he was saying her name right.

"Born and raised," she said, looking around quickly as if to make sure her supervisor wasn't watching. Then she relaxed a bit and nodded. "How about you?"

The Sheikh laughed. "Thank Allah, no! I cannot even stand a chilly breeze, let alone blocks of ice falling from the sky."

"It's just a snowstorm," said Willow. "Though it is looking pretty rough out there. I hope you weren't planning on leaving anytime soon."

The Sheikh frowned. "What do you mean? I have a meeting in New York City in two days."

Willow raised her eyebrows. "Well, you could start driving tonight and you might make it in two days. Assuming you have a truck, of course. And even then it'll be slow going across the Midwest. It's supposed to come down heavy for two straight days, and then it'll take a while to get the roads cleared."

"I do not care about the roads so long as the runways are clear," said the Sheikh, frowning as he glanced at his watch and wondered if he should call his pilots and see if they could take off tonight itself, before this storm got any worse—as if it was possible for the storm to get any worse.

"I'm pretty sure all flights have been grounded. I'd be surprised if the airport is even open. I have a couple of friends who work ground crew for one of the airlines, and they couldn't make it out past their own driveways!"

"I do not care about the airlines. I have my own airplane."

"Yeah, but if there's no air-traffic controllers and no one to plow the runways, then it doesn't matter. You aren't going anywhere. I'd suggest extending your hotel reservation now, just to make sure you're not stuck without a room." Willow glanced over the crowd. "Not sure how many of these folks are out-of-towners, but they're all gonna be extending their stays through Thanksgiving." She snorted. "And I hope you've already got your turkey, because there might be a run on birds at the grocery store."

The woman went quiet for a moment, as if something had occurred to her. She blinked, her eyes narrowing a bit as she glanced down at him. If this were any other woman, the Sheikh would have thought she was checking him out. But this felt different. It was like she was evaluating him, making an assessment, judging his worthiness or something. Whatever. He had bigger things to think about. Like how the hell he was going to get out of here.

"Turkey?" he said absentmindedly as he glanced at the window and wondered if it was his imagination or if the snowflakes really looked as big as frozen turkeys. "Thanksgiving?"

"You're kidding, right? You know it's Thanksgiving on Thursday. Tell me you know what Thanksgiving is!"

The Sheikh shifted on his chair. "Of course I do."

"You ever been to an American Thanksgiving?"

"No," said Rafeez. "Why? Are you inviting me to your home, Miss Willow?"

Willow laughed. "I'll be working on Thanksgiving. I get paid time and a half on holidays. But if you're still in town . . ."

She trailed off, and the Sheikh could tell from the way she hesitated that whatever she'd thought about earlier was still playing on her mind. Now he was curious, and he turned on his chair and looked up at the short-haired woman. "Go on, Miss Willow. What should I do if I am stuck in town for Thanksgiving?"

"You should get your own bird. A local, North Dakota turkey. I have a friend who runs a turkey farm just outside Fargo. If you've got a four-wheel drive vehicle, you should be able to get there." She smiled, her eyes sparkling as if there was some inside joke that the Sheikh wasn't getting—or wouldn't get until later. "Tell her you want to buy her largest turkey, and that you want her to stuff it for you."

The Sheikh laughed. "A fine idea. But I am staying in a hotel. What in Allah's name am I going to do with a stuffed turkey? Cook it in the microwave in my suite?"

Willow shrugged. "I'm sure you guys will figure something out." She smiled again, turning to go get the Sheikh his club soda. "Oh, and tell her Willow sent you."

# 3

"Of course she did," said Pen, blinking twice as she stared up at the tall, dark-haired man standing in her doorway. He wore a thick leather jacket with a fur-lined collar, and Pen frowned as she wondered which poor animal had been shaved to line this man's collar. But she couldn't hold the thought for long, because the man's green eyes were locked in on hers with a cool confidence that made her feel warm all over, tingly beneath her clothes, hot between her legs.

Willow had sent her a cryptic text saying she was sending over a "customer" and that Pen should keep her hair open and not in that ratty ponytail. What the hell did that mean, Pen had wondered. But then, on the Wednesday before Thanksgiving, the doorchimes had gone wild and when she pulled the door open she saw the man standing there.

It was clear what Willow had done, and one look into his twinkling green eyes and half-formed smile told Pen that this man knew it too. She almost swooned as she took in the sight of his strong jawline highlighted by perfectly manicured stubble, thick black hair that complemented his smooth olive skin, dark red lips so full and thick Pen had to force herself not to think about where she wanted to feel their warmth.

Her mind spun a web of doubt, excitement, and straight-up panic as Pen wondered what the hell to do next. Clearly Willow had decided she was going to send over this man as some misguided attempt at matchmaking. Absolutely misguided, Pen thought as she touched her hair and felt her right leg bend back involuntarily like she was a stork or something.

I hate you, Willow, she thought as she swallowed and tried to fight the feeling that this guy was way out of her league. I hate you, and I love you. Oh, God, I love you so much, you dark-haired little witch!

"So Willow sent you here to buy a turkey," she said slowly, feeling the cool air swirl up around her black tights, which she was wearing beneath a long, hip-hugging maroon sweater that highlighted her curves while nicely hiding the round of her belly. "But it sounds like we're the turkeys here."

The man raised an eyebrow and pulled his fur-lined collar closer. "May I come in?" he said. His accent sent a chill through her, its Middle Eastern lilt tempered by a vague hint of British propriety. It sounded almost royal, Pen thought. Which was ridiculous, of course. There weren't any royals anymore, were there? And certainly none that would show up at her door in a obvious set-up situation!

But why did he show up, anyway, Pen wondered as she stared tongue-tied into his eyes, blinking as she glanced at his mouth again, horrified as she pushed away an image of those lips of his between her legs, his tongue sliding out and disappearing into her—

Oh, God, are you insane, she thought, blinking again and stepping back so the man could enter. There were snowflakes all over his thick locks of hair and massively broad shoulders, and when he took off his jacket and stomped his feet in her foyer, she almost gasped out loud when she saw how big his chest looked in the tight-fitting black cashmere sweater he wore.

"OK, this is awkward," Pen said as the blood rushed to her face. Suddenly she felt very white and exposed, and she unconsciously tugged at the bottom of her long sweater, wondering if she going to start sweating. Had she used enough deodorant? Had she used too much perfume? Was her lipstick too thick? And again, why would a man like this even show up to what was in effect a blind date? "The next time I see Willow, I'm gonna . . ."

"She is a good friend to you. I trusted her immediately, and that is why I am here," said the man, looking her straight on with a calm confidence that shook Pen to the core. He winked. "Though of course my bodyguards are outside, just in case you try any funny stuff. I am not that kind of man, you know."

"Of course not," Pen said, surprising herself by how confident she sounded while inside she was a quivering mess of high-school level nerves. "And I'm not that kind of woman."

The Sheikh took a step closer, and Pen could smell his scent: red sage and desert oak, a mix so potent that she touched her neck as she inhaled deep. "What kind of woman are you?" he asked, his half-smile breaking into a full grin as Pen wondered what the hell was happening, what was going to happen, and what in God's name she'd do if he took one more step.

"The kind who invites strange men into her home, obviously," she said, blushing as the thought came to her that this man was twice her size, and she was alone in this old farmhouse. No one would hear her scream. She had a shotgun, but it was in the cellar, and she hadn't cleaned or fired it in years. What the hell was Willow thinking!

What the hell am *I* thinking, Pen wondered as she reminded herself that Willow wasn't particularly

*Grateful for the Sheikh*

good at long-term planning or thinking too many steps ahead. The woman operated mostly on instinct, and although that had worked out reasonably well in Willow's life—she was married to a nice woman and they'd adopted twins from South America—Pen wasn't so sure if those instincts would carry over when it came to Pen's life.

And then suddenly she decided this was ridiculous, that she couldn't handle it, that she needed to turn her back on it—whatever it was! What the hell was this guy doing in Fargo, anyway? No way he lived here. Which meant that no way he was looking for anything more than . . .

"The turkey," he said, raising an eyebrow and looking around as if he expected to see rows of dead birds hanging in her damned living room. "This is a turkey farm, yes?"

Pen blinked and folded her arms beneath her breasts, almost fainting when she saw how his gaze shamelessly moved to her bosom for a long moment before he looked back up into her eyes. "OK, Willow was messing with you. With me, I mean. With us, I guess."

"How is that? I do not understand."

"Well, this was always a turkey farm, and it still is, in a way. But after my parents passed a few years ago, I stopped . . . well, I don't . . . I mean, these turkeys aren't for eating."

The Sheikh frowned. "What are they for?"

Pen frowned right back. "They aren't *for* anything! They're living things, creatures of this world. They're just alive! They're just—"

"Ya Allah," the Sheikh groaned, rubbing his forehead and looking down. "Please do not tell me you are a peace-loving vegetarian who believes that eating meat is some form of barbaric activity, akin to murder."

Pen put her hands on her hips, feeling the blood rise in her—and not in the way it had risen earlier when she'd seen his tall, muscular frame in her doorway. "You say that as if it's laughable to not want to murder innocent animals just to stuff your damned face!" she said, her frown getting deeper. She knew every little line on her face was probably visible right now, but she didn't give a damn. There was something about the lazy, flippant way in which he'd pretty much dismissed everything she believed in with one mocking sentence that made her decide she wasn't sleeping with him if he was the last man on Earth.

And that's when she imagined Willow standing triumphantly in the background, grinning like an elf, pointing out the annoying little tidbit that if Pen was hotly deciding that she'd *never* sleep with this man, it simply proved that all she'd been thinking about since this man walked into her home was . . .

"How do you sleep with all that noise?" the man asked, cocking his head.

"What noise?" said Pen. She listened, and then she realized that although the birds were housed a hundred yards away, you still could hear them fluttering and gobbling and doing whatever it was that turkeys did when no one was watching. She laughed and shook her head. "I guess it's always just been background noise for me, and I just tuned it out."

The man nodded. "The soundtrack of your life, yes? Gobble gobble."

"Excuse me?" Pen said, suddenly feeling self-conscious. "Did you just call me fat?"

"What?" said the man, and for the first time Pen saw him look flustered as the color rushed to his brown face. "Of course not! I do not comment on a woman's appearance! That was not what I meant at all!"

Pen closed her eyes and bit her lip. She really knew how to step in it, didn't she. "No, of course not. I don't know why I said that. I'm just nervous, I guess."

"I make you nervous?"

Pen blinked as she studied his handsome face, which had regained its natural, almost regal composure. "No," she said finally. "It's not you. It's the situation, I suppose. I haven't dated in a long time, and—"

The man raised an eyebrow, his green eyes shining with mischief. "So this is a date? How very curious. Please, go on."

Pen went so red she was certain she could blend in with a bowl of tomatoes. "No," she said hurriedly, touching her hair as her eyelids fluttered involuntarily. "I mean, it's . . . oh, God, I don't even know what I'm saying. How about we start over? I'm Penelope Peterson," she said, sticking out an arm awkwardly.

"Rafeez Al-Zahaar," said the man, making no move to shake her hand. "And there is no starting over. This is perfect."

"What's perfect?"

The man snorted, holding his arms out wide and making a slow turn around her living room. "This. All of it. This place. This week. This trip. All of it. A perfect mess."

"Mess?" said Pen, feeling her frown coming on again as she tried to fight it back. "So first you call me fat, and now you're saying my place is a mess?"

"Ya Allah," said Rafeez, rubbing his heavy stubble and grinning, showing off his perfectly aligned, naturally white teeth. "You are putting words in my mouth."

And I'm putting my fat foot in my own mouth, thought Pen. But she could feel some of the awkwardness start to melt away even as they both laughed hesitantly. This actually does feel like an awkward first date, she thought as she felt her blush come on again but without her caring this time. She brushed away a strand of hair from her cheek and glanced up into his eyes, feeling that telltale heat whip through her when she saw the look in his eyes.

Then suddenly she didn't care that this man Rafeez probably didn't live in Fargo, perhaps didn't even live in the United States at all. She just cared that he was making her tights feel tight, her panties feel wet, and her bra feel damned uncomfortable, like it needed to be taken off and tossed across her "messy" living room.

It's Thanksgiving, she thought as she stared into the handsome stranger's green eyes and shifted on her feet as she felt the connection between them grow even as she sensed movement at the front of his fitted trousers. It's Thanksgiving, and Willow has sent you a gift, you moron. So just accept it and be grateful. Be grateful.

To hell with it, she thought as she watched Rafeez take a step toward her like he knew what she was thinking, knew that she was saying yes, knew that she wanted what he wanted. It's storming outside, and chances are when it clears up you'll never see this man again. So to hell with it. Just go with it.

She felt herself nod, the movement so subtle she wasn't sure if it was real or not, if it meant anything or not. Then she felt his body near hers, his arm sliding around her back, his strength drawing her in, his scent overwhelming her senses as she gasped and looked up into his eyes.

And when he kissed her, she closed those eyes and gave thanks.

Thank you, she said as she kissed him back, opening her mouth and letting him in. Thank you for this.

# 4

Is this what I came here for, the Sheikh thought as he felt the thrill of the kiss rip through his body like a sandstorm. The kiss was gentle, but the waves of passion that stirred inside him were building to where the Sheikh could barely breathe as he kissed her again, pulling her close against his body, his right arm tight around the small of her back, his left hand sliding around to her ass and squeezing firmly.

Soon he was grinding his cock against her crotch, and he grinned against her cheek as he felt her pull her thick sweater up slightly to give him access to her front. He reached between them and rubbed her gently with the back of his hand, pushing his knuckles against her mound as he drove his tongue into her mouth. Their kisses were gaining intensity, and the Sheikh could sense a desperation in the way they were touching, a deep-seated yearning in the way their bodies were rubbing against each other. Perhaps it was the cold outside that made him yearn for her heat like this. Perhaps it was something else. Who the hell knew. All he knew was that this was happening, and it was perfect. Just bloody perfect!

"You are perfect," he muttered, pulling her sweater up over her head, his eyes almost rolling back in his head at the sight of her magnificent breasts barely contained by the beige satin bra. "Ya Allah, I am so bloody hard for you. I do not know what has come over me."

"Oh, so other women don't get you hard?" she whispered, and the Sheikh snorted with surprised laughter as he pulled back from the kiss and looked upon her face. She was blushing, her eyes wide with embarrassment. "Oh, shit. I didn't mean that! I meant . . . OK, I'm just gonna shut up now."

The Sheikh leaned his head back and laughed out loud. "Perfect," he said again. "A perfect mess. Come here, Miss Vegetarian Turkey Farmer. Come to me."

"I think I'm about as close as I can get," Pen said, raising an eyebrow and then looking down at their bodies smushed together as the Sheikh placed both palms firmly on the rounds of her buttocks and squeezed hard. "Oh, God, that feels good."

"I think we can get closer," Rafeez whispered, kissing her forehead, her nose, her cheeks, even her damned eyelids. He pushed his hands down inside her tights and underwear, his cock going to full mast as he ran his fingers along the smooth skin of her ass, pulling her cheeks apart and touching her crack as she gasped and shuddered under his grip. "Still so much cloth between us. Come, we'd better get you out of these."

She nodded earnestly, looking down at herself as she placed her hands on his chest to steady herself. "We'd better, yes. Too much cloth."

The Sheikh went down on his knees in a flash, gripping the waistband of her tights and ripping it apart with such force she yelped in surprise, her hands grabbing his thick hair as he pulled the tattered Spandex off her. Then he tore her panties off by the side seam, smacking her thick thighs with his open palms, making her yelp again as he inhaled deep of her feminine scent.

"Spread for me," he said, rubbing her thighs and calves and gently pulling so she took a wider stance before him. "A little more. Open up so I can taste you. Ah, yes. That is good. Perfect. Ya Allah, you smell so good. I must taste you."

"Oh . . . oh, shit," he heard her mutter from above him, her hands pulling at his hair as he nuzzled her pubic curls with his nose and then slowly began to lick her slit with long, forceful strokes. She smelled clean and fresh, tasted tangy and sweet, and the Sheikh could barely control his need as he rubbed her thighs and pushed his face deep between them.

He reached down with one hand so he could unbuckle and unzip. His cock was so big and hard he could barely breathe from the feeling of being restricted by his underwear and trousers. Somehow he managed to get his pants off while still keeping his face pushed up in her crotch as she clawed at his hair and rubbed her mound all over his nose and mouth.

Rafeez could feel her juices coating his stubble, dripping down his chin, and he grinned as he finally pulled his trousers and underwear down to his muscular thighs, releasing his cock. It sprung out straight ahead of him, and he stroked it and shuddered, wondering if he'd ever been this hard, this thick, this full of desire for a woman.

"Never," he muttered as he let go of his erection out of fear he would come too soon. "Ya Allah, never!"

"What's that?" she groaned from above him. "What?"

"Never mind," he answered, grinning as he licked her dark lips and tasted her sweet tang. "Come. Come down here with me."

"I think I'm already coming," she muttered, and he could feel her buttocks quivering as he pulled her rear cheeks apart and ran his fingers along her crack, pushing his tongue deep into her cunt as he did it, curling it upwards and driving it against the fibrous point of her g-spot. "Oh, *shit*! What is that! What are you doing to me?! Oh, *God*!"

He felt her come all over his face, and he licked and sucked as hard as he could, pushing his middle finger into her rear hole as he did it. She screamed as she came again, and when she pushed her crotch against his face and began to grind shamelessly, with abandon, like she'd lost herself, did not care for anything but the way he was making her feel, the Sheikh knew he couldn't hold back any longer.

With a roar he pulled her down to the floor with him, catching her with his strong arms as her knees buckled. He pushed her down onto her back, raising her arms above her head, sucking and biting at her creamy, heavy breasts, her big red nipples as she moaned and thrashed beneath him.

She was clearly still coming as the Sheikh rammed his cock into her, and he groaned out loud as he felt her heat envelop his hardness, her wetness coat his shaft as he began to drive and pump into her with a frenzy that he didn't know he had in him.

"Ya Allah," he gasped as he felt his cock somehow expand within her until he knew he was stretching her walls to their limit, opening her up to the max, penetrating her deeper than any man had, than any man could. "I have never felt this kind of need for a woman!"

"Oh, so it's been a while for you too, huh?" she said, looking up at him, her brown eyes big and innocent as she teased him.

The Sheikh roared with laughter, his eyes wide with surprise at the playfulness of this woman spread beneath him, her beautiful curves taking everything his body had to give.

"I am so aroused I do not even remember who or what I slept with before you," he shot back, flexing his cock inside her. He pulled halfway out and drove back in with all the force he had, gritting his teeth when he saw Pen's eyes roll up in her head as her body shuddered with the impact of his re-entry. "But think very carefully about making these kinds of jokes again, my little farmgirl." He pushed his hands beneath her ass, lifting her thighs and grinning as she wrapped her heavy legs around him. He kept pumping as he managed to claw his fingers around to her crack once more, firmly planting his thumb on her rear pucker as he felt her shudder again as her next orgasm became imminent.

Then suddenly the Sheikh stopped, driving his cock deep and holding still as a rock. He looked into her eyes as she opened them and stared up at him, her body still shuddering. "Be careful," he whispered, still grinning as he pushed his thumb into her ass from beneath, flexing his cock again, kissing her lips gently and then drawing his head back to look at her. "Be very careful."

Suddenly her eyes flicked wide open, and he felt her push against his tight chest. "Oh, shit," she said. "I'm not on birth control! You need to pull out! What am I doing! I can't do this!"

The Sheikh frowned as a chill ran along his spine. Ya Allah, he had not even thought of that! How could that be? He was usually extraordinarily careful about where he put his royal cock! He had a dozen condoms in his trouser pocket, but yet he had not even considered reaching for one. The desire to feel her from the inside had been too strong, and now there was a desire to come inside her too—a need so primal, so deep, so uncontrollable that it scared him.

I want to feel my seed pouring into her, Rafeez realized as he felt his balls tighten even though the two of them were still like statues. And why not? It is the most natural thing, is it not? The most basic need of a man? And what is the risk, truly? The chances of her getting pregnant from one encounter are low in general, yes? Who knows where she is in her cycle. Who knows how fertile she is. And what is the worst case? That she actually does get pregnant? So what? So bloody what?

Slowly the Sheikh began pumping again, even though he knew it was madness. He'd met this woman less than an hour ago. She was about as far away from a suitable candidate to be Sheikha as one could think of! There could never be anything between them, and here he was about to pour his royal seed into her!

"No, you need to pull out, Rafeez," she whispered, pushing harder against his chest. "Listen, you need to—"

Suddenly the Sheikh felt a rush of anger whip through him. "No one tells me what I *need* to do, understood? I am a goddamn king and I will do as I please. I will come where I want. As often as I want." He kept pumping as he felt his heavy balls slap against her from below. "And do not pretend for my benefit. Any woman would jump at the chance to be—"

He did not finish the sentence, because his face exploded in pain as she slapped him clean across the cheek, sending the blood rushing to his head so fast he shouted in surprised anger.

"Get the hell off me, you arrogant piece of shit!" she said, almost spitting the words out. She brought her hand back to slap him again, but the Sheikh grabbed both her wrists and pinned them up over her head, pushing all his weight flat against her body so she couldn't move at all. "Stop, or I'll scream!"

"Bloody right you will scream," the Sheikh grunted, clenching his jaw as he narrowed his eyes and stared at her as he felt a manic surge of energy course through his hard body. "Because I will make you scream. I will make you scream for more."

Still holding her wrists above her, her body securely held down by his weight, the Sheikh looked around the room. His gaze fell on the tattered Spandex of her black tights which he'd ripped down the seam, and he grinned and reached for them. He twisted the black cloth around her wrists, testing its strength as he pulled it tight.

"What are you doing?" she gasped, her brown eyes wide as she stared up at him. "This isn't funny."

"Really? Because I am laughing. See?" said the Sheikh, grinning wide as he tied the ends of her bindings around the leg of the heavy oakwood dining table that he was confident she wouldn't be able to lift while she was on the floor. He tied the knots and then without hesitation got off her and flipped her over, pulling her ass up in the air and smacking her rump hard with his open palm. "Now scream if you want. Scream for me while I laugh!"

He spanked her again, watching her heavy buttocks quiver with the force of his slaps. He could see the smooth, creamy skin turn red, with fingermarks appearing on her magnificent globes as she howled and pulled on her bindings.

"You're a psycho!" she screamed, turning her head and trying to kick out at him. But the Sheikh held her legs down, smacking the back of her thighs, making her howl again as she got the message and stopped kicking out.

"I was not until I met you," he whispered, slowing down suddenly and beginning to rub her buttocks. He kissed her smooth asscheeks, sliding his hand between her thighs. "Ya Allah, you are wet. So damned wet."

He felt her shudder with arousal as he ran his fingers along her slit, feeling her wetness coat his hands down to the wrist. He kept kissing her rear globes, taking his mouth closer and closer to her divine crack until he was licking her up and down as he felt her relax and begin to spread for him.

"So yet another wanton woman has turned a good, decent man into a psycho rapist?" she muttered, arching her back down as the Sheikh pushed two fingers into her cunt from below. "Funny how that happens."

"I am sorry," he whispered from between her rear cheeks. "I lost control. It has never happened before, I swear it."

"Oh, you *swear* it!" she said, mocking his accent in a way that made Rafeez want to spank her again. "Well, that makes me feel a lot better. You realize I'm still tied to my own damned table, and you're . . . you're . . . oh, God, what are you doing. Yes, do that. Keep doing that. Oh, *shit*!"

The Sheikh slid his tongue into her rear hole, curling three fingers in her pussy as he did it, and he could feel her come instantly. He kept up the dual penetration, feeling his cock yearning to re-enter her. He was dripping pre-cum all over the floorboards, and he was surprised he hadn't blown his load yet. But somehow he knew his seed belonged in this woman, and he was finishing inside her, one way or the other.

"All right," he gasped, finally pulling his tongue out of her asshole as he felt her climax peak and then slowly wind down as she convulsed under his touch. "To show you I am sorry and that I am not a psycho rapist, as you so eloquently suggested, I will let you choose. I am finishing inside you, one way or another. One place or another. But you can decide where. I am a gentleman, and I will let the lady make the choice."

"What choice?" she muttered, clearly still out of her senses from how hard she'd come.

"The choice about where I put my seed, little farm-girl. Which opening? Quickly now. I cannot wait much longer. Choose, or I will choose for you."

# 5

*Choose or I will choose for you.*

Pen wasn't sure if this was a dream or a nightmare. She'd already come more times than she could count, and although Rafeez had scared the hell out of her for a moment, that moment had passed. If anything, the fear had heightened her need, even though she hated to admit it. Although it sounded laughable, she actually did believe that he'd lost control in a way he never had before. After all, *she'd* certainly lost control in a way she never had, right? Hell, he was doing things to her she'd never even fantasized about, and she was wet and hot, coming like some slut under his erotic touch.

I'll get you for this, Willow, she thought as she smiled at the filthy choice this man had put forth. She tugged at her bindings, feeling the table move a little as she pulled. If she really wanted she could get up on her knees and lift the table enough to slip her bound hands free. She could probably even pull the knot open with her teeth. But there was something about being tied up like a prisoner, spanked like a bad girl, fucked like a whore that was speaking to a part of Pen that she didn't know existed.

Maybe it's this storm, she thought, trying to reason with herself, come to terms with why she was enjoying this so much, even when she was afraid of this muscular, dark man with a thick Arabian accent and an even thicker cock. Yeah, that's it. The storm. It's cast this dark shadow on everything, making things seem surreal, making it seem like everything's upside down, turned around, twisted like how my poor torn tights are twisted around my wrists.

"Hurry up, little farmgirl," he whispered from behind her, running his finger down along her spine as she shivered and gasped. "Choose, or I will choose for you. And I am so full and ready, I may fill all three of your holes if you do not choose."

The thought of this stranger coming everywhere, in every opening, pouring his load into her mouth, pussy, and anus almost made her come again, and she closed her eyes and groaned as the Sheikh's finger stopped at the small of her back, just above the ridge of her ass.

"All right. All right! Just give me a moment," she whispered, arching her back down and turning her head halfway. A part of her wanted to suck him, swallow him, let him pour his heat down her throat. But she couldn't deny that when he'd pushed his fingers into her rear she'd been aroused in the most filthy, sick way . . . a way she never imagined was possible, a way she suspected wouldn't be possible with any other man. The very thought of taking a man there, of letting a man go there, of letting a man come there had been so off-limits in her mind that she hadn't even toyed with the idea. But now, after an hour with this beast from the East, she was tied and spread, about to actually *choose* to have him enter where no man had gone before!

"You know," he said, tracing little circles with his fingertip on the small of her back, slowly moving down along her asscrack as she shuddered. "Any other woman would have let me come inside her pussy. Any other woman would have begged me to fill her with my royal seed. But you shout at me to pull out, and when I do not, you slap me across the face!" He grunted as he ran his hand sideways along her crack gently. Then he pulled his hand back and smacked her bottom again, doing it twice on each cheek and then stopping. "You do not understand who I am, do you?"

*Grateful for the Sheikh*

Pen swallowed hard as she waited for the stinging to subside. Then she turned her head to the side and raised an eyebrow. "I understand that you're a typical man suffering from the delusion that every woman you sleep with wants to carry your lovechild. It's a sickness, you know. Extreme narcissism. Exemplified by the fact that you called yourself a king earlier. A king! In Fargo, North Dakota!"

Rafeez laughed out loud, smacking her ass again and then leaning forward and kissing her lower back. "Do you know what the title Sheikh means?"

Pen shrugged. "It means Mister or Sir in the Middle East."

"It means *king*, my little American farmgirl," he whispered from down near her back. "I am Sheikh Rafeez Al-Zahaar. King Rafeez of Zahaar. *King* of Zahaar!"

"I'm *so* impressed," Pen said, not quite sure what to make of him. He sounded serious, but delusional people *were* serious. That's what delusional meant! "And what is Zaa-haar? Your playground where you built sandcastles as a kid? Then you declared yourself king of the sandpit and now you hang out in North Dakota and try to knock women up with your self-proclaimed royal seed? You know, I've met some weirdoes in my life, but you're by far the—"

But she didn't finish her sentence, because she felt a cool breeze around her bare ankles and thighs.

Then she heard the front door slam, and as she turned her head in a panic, wondering if someone else had walked in, her heart almost stopped when she realized the room was empty. She was alone. Her king was gone. He'd walked right out the damned door without saying another word! He'd just up and left!

Pen frowned as the pit in her stomach expanded to where she could barely breathe. She thought she was going to be sick, and she couldn't understand why!

But as she went up on her knees and pulled up the heavy table just enough to slide the tights out and free herself, she forced herself to acknowledge that she knew exactly why she felt sick. This man had walked into her life, sent to her by Willow, a gift from her best friend. And Pen had driven him away, insulted and mocked him to the point where she must have hurt his pride.

"When will you learn to keep your big fat mouth *shut*?!" she screamed, not sure why she was screaming. She sat there on her haunches, naked and vulnerable, wondering if the door would open again and he'd come rushing in like an Arabian stallion, push her down face-first, punish her for her rudeness, then take what he wanted, the way a king takes what he wants, how he wants. Finally she wondered if she *wanted* him to come back, or if this was for the best. After all, he'd tied her up, spanked her nice and hard, and then threatened to take her in every opening! Who knew what this man was capable of?! Who knew where his cock had been before her?!

But what upset her most was the sinking thought that who knew where this would have led if she'd just kept her big fat mouth *shut*!

Slowly Pen reached for her sweater and pulled it on. It was long enough to get past her hips, and she pulled it down without bothering to find her bra and panties—though if she remembered right, the Sheikh had ripped both those just like he'd destroyed her tights.

I should send him a bill for my underwear and tights, she thought, frowning as she held up the tattered black Spandex. These are Lulu Lemons. Not cheap.

Whatever, she thought, laughing and tossing the useless tights aside. She reached for her phone, checking the time and deciding it wasn't too late to call Willow and give the bitch a piece of her mind. Or thank her. Pen wasn't sure which.

"Hello?" she said, frowning when an unfamiliar male voice answered Willow's phone. She pulled her phone back from her ear and checked the screen to make sure she'd dialed right. She had, and so she got back on and said hello again. "Who is this? Why do you have Willow's phone?"

"Are you related to Ms. Willow?" came the voice, and Pen felt a chill run through her when she heard a flurry of voices and random electronic sounds in the background. It sounded like an emergency room at a hospital, came the thought, and Pen almost choked as she managed to control herself long enough to respond.

"I'm her best friend, the godmother of her children, and I was her emergency contact until she got married three years ago," she said in the most serious tone she could muster. "You need to tell me what's happening."

There was a pause, and then the man spoke again. "Your friend's been in a car accident." He paused again, lowering his voice as he went on. "That's all I can tell you." Another long pause, and then the man's tone changed, and what he said next told Pen everything she needed to know. "I'm sorry," he said. "I'm really, really sorry."

# 6

"We're so sorry to make you all attend a funeral on Thanksgiving Day. And knowing Willow, she'd have been sorry too."

A few polite chuckles and some murmurs rose up from the small crowd gathered at Parson's Funeral Home in Fargo. The funeral director had given a short, respectful speech, and now Willow's spouse Randy was up at the podium, her eyes red and bloodshot but her face smooth with makeup. Randy spoke haltingly, and Pen frowned and shook her head as she tried not to stand up and say, "Hell yes, Willow would have been sorry! There's no reason to have the funeral on Thanksgiving Day, you attention-hog! Willow's not going anywhere! She's already gone! The funeral could have waited for the day after Thanksgiving, yeah?"

"But knowing Willow," Randy added, doubling down on her joke, "she'd have been more sorry to make you all come in on Black Friday and miss out on the shopping deals!"

Pen winced and rubbed her forehead. Willow hated shopping, and she'd always rolled her eyes at the folks who lined up outside Target or Sears at the crack of dawn for all the Day-After-Thanksgiving sales. She wouldn't have felt any regret for making people wear black and dab their eyes politely at Parson's Funeral Home instead of buying another oversized television set!

OK, you've got to calm the hell down, Pen told herself, dabbing her own damned eyes and wondering how much more of this awkward speech she could take. Randy's handling this by making bad jokes, and you're handling this by getting angry that Randy doesn't know Willow as well as you knew her. But that's to be expected, isn't it? Hell, you've known Willow since the two of you were teenagers! You knew her when she was still fucking men! You were the first one she called after she'd slept with a woman the first time! You were maid of honor and best bitch at her wedding! And you think it should be you giving the eulogy, don't you?

But Randy is her spouse, and that's how it goes,

Pen told herself. You'll have your chance to give your speech when they open it up to the floor. What does it matter who goes first? Willow wouldn't care. Willow would know it was you that came first. Willow *does* know.

She does, Pen told herself as she glanced up at the dark yellow ceiling of the funeral home. She could feel the tears streaking her makeup, and she dabbed her face again and then stood and made her way to the restroom. She could hear the crowd reward Randy with another round of awkward chuckles, and she stared at her reflection in the mirror and shook her head. She was about to burst into tears, but then she smiled instead.

Maybe Randy made the right choice having the funeral on Thanksgiving, it suddenly occurred to her, and as she thought it her heart filled to the point where she worried it might burst. She nodded at herself again, smiled so wide it hurt, and took a deep, sighing breath. Then she went back out to the main room, waited politely for Randy to finish, and finally stepped up to the podium without bothering to pull out the speech she'd carefully written the previous night.

"Be grateful," she said. "Not sad, but grateful. Grateful that you had those times with Willow. Grateful that she was ever in your life. Grateful that she didn't suffer much in death. Be grateful. Grateful for everything that Willow brought into your life. Be grateful. That's all I have to say."

Pen blinked as she stared at the faces in the crowd. Then she blinked again as another face came to mind, a face that Willow had brought into Pen's life—*sent* into Pen's life. A face that Pen would never see again.

Good riddance, Pen thought as she finished what she had to say and stepped away from the podium. I don't *want* to see that weirdo again, anyway. Who acts like that?! Who goes from being charismatic and funny to becoming a goddamn madman and then suddenly shuts down and leaves?! To hell with him! I'm grateful he's *gone*!

The rest of the funeral was a blur of tiny sandwiches, lemonade, and hot tea, and Pen smiled and shook hands and thanked people for their compliments on her speech. She hugged Randy and Willow's twins, quietly reminding them she was their godmother and would always be there for them, no matter what. They barely understood what was happening. They'd only been adopted a few years earlier from Colombia, and all of it probably still seemed like a dream to them. Pen was sad they wouldn't ever get to know Willow as they grew up, but she was grateful because the loss might hurt less. Those kids had been through enough, losing their own parents in a freak accident when they were caught in the crossfire during a shootout between Colombian Police and the Colombian Drug Cartel.

But as Pen slowly drove home alone, navigating through icy patches on the road, glancing at snowbanks that rose six feet high on the sidewalks and shoulders, she couldn't help see the Sheikh's face in her mind's eye, feel his touch on her body, smell his masculine scent in the air. They'd had a connection, hadn't they? And he probably though *she* was a weirdo-freak for those dumb comments she'd made: "Was Zahaar your imaginary playground where you built sandcastles and declared yourself king?"

A king, Pen thought as she frowned and wondered if that could be true. She didn't know a lot about the Middle East, and she'd assumed that most countries didn't have kings and queens anymore. But there was something about Rafeez, the way he'd carried himself, his lazy, cool confidence, his expensive, tailored clothes, that heavy, diamond-studded watch. And hadn't he said he had bodyguards waiting outside? She'd assumed it was just a joke, but he'd said it matter-of-factly—yes, as part of a joke; but the joke wasn't about the bodyguards.

Shit, tell me I didn't just insult some whacko Arab king, Pen thought as she got home and rushed indoors to her computer, furiously typing in all the spellings of "Rafeez" and "Zahaar" she could think of until finally she gasped and smacked herself on the forehead when she got a Wikipedia entry for "Sheikh Rafeez, leader of the Kingdom of Zahaar."

She raced through the article, her eyes burning as her mind whirled from the memories of what had happened on her living room floor just a day ago.

"Oil billionaire. Only child and sole heir to the throne. Educated in Dubai, Saudi Arabia, and England," she muttered as she read, her head shaking involuntarily as she pushed aside the thought that this oil billionaire had been about to knock her up and she'd slapped him across the damned face and told him to pull out!

Pen almost laughed out loud when she realized what she was thinking. And then she was ashamed for thinking it. She hated herself for thinking it. But she couldn't help it, and finally she just said screw it and let the fantasy wash over her: North Dakota woman pregnant from a casual encounter with an Arabian Sheikh! What happens next?! OMG!

Sounds like a teaser for a cheesy *Mills and Boon* romance, Pen thought as she heard the telltale sounds of her birds getting restless for their feeding. She smiled and pushed aside the fantasy even as she realized she was wet beneath her black slacks, her cotton panties soaked in a way that surprised her because she hadn't noticed she was aroused. Still smiling, she grabbed her coat and headed out to her birds.

Of course, she told herself with a touch of melancholy, nobody writes a Sheikh romance where the heroine is a vegetarian turkey farmer with a fat ass.

# 7

**R**afeez pushed aside the thought of her beautiful round ass as he watched the sand dunes roll by. He'd been out hunting for desert fowl, but he'd come up short. Not a bird in sight. It was almost like they'd fled his kingdom. Flown South for the winter or something.

The Sheikh smiled tightly as he glanced toward the sun through the heavily tinted, bulletproof windows of his gold Range Rover. The car moved silently through the desert, the driver maneuvering along the crests of the dunes, navigating by GPS as the caravan of Range Rovers made their way from the open

*Grateful for the Sheikh*

sands towards the paved road that would take them back to Zahaar's Capital City.

Soon Rafeez caught sight of the tallest minarets of Zahaar rising up on the horizon. He'd always thought those minarets looked like a sea of erections popping out of the desert: straight, thick shafts with a head on top. He smiled again as he wondered what his people would think if they knew that their exalted Sheikh's thoughts were perpetually focused on one thing and one thing only.

"Well, two things," Rafeez muttered, clenching his fists as he thought of that "little" farmgirl's big, beautiful rear globes. He could feel himself get hard, and he shifted on the smooth white leather seat as he closed his eyes and took a deep breath. He could almost taste the sweetness between her legs, smell her thick feminine musk as he imagined pushing his face back between her thighs. Why had he not finished what he'd started? She'd aroused him in a way he'd never experienced in even his wildest, most memorable sexual encounters, and yet he'd abruptly ended the encounter without climaxing!

Stop it, the Sheikh told himself, shifting again in his seat as his erection made his pants so tight he winced. You are obsessed. It is not healthy. She is just a woman. One of many in your past. One of many more to come. Forget her. She means nothing. *Nothing*!

Rafeez closed his eyes and inhaled deep, trying to push the image of Penelope Peterson out of his mind. But she was lodged in there, and the Sheikh clenched his fists tighter and shook his head as they approached the outskirts of Zahaar's Capital City.

I should have finished what I started, the Sheikh thought as he glanced absentmindedly at a new shopping mall that was under construction. There were construction projects underway all over the city—part of the Sheikh's efforts to invite foreign investment. Indeed, that had been the reason he'd agreed to attend Charlotte's wedding—to raise his profile in the West, perhaps get the Kingdom of Zahaar mentioned in academic and political circles as being an up-and-coming nation that was safe to invest in because its ruler was not a fanatical nutcase.

Rafeez went through the sequence of events once again: The phone call from Charlotte. His decision to fly to North Dakota. The snowstorm. That conversation with the short-haired caterer. And then a blind date with a turkey farmer!

The Sheikh frowned as he thought back to his fruitless hunting trip in the desert. The desert fowl he usually hunted for sport were flightless birds that were a distant cousin of the North American turkey. He frowned again, rubbing his stubble as a strange thought began to take form.

Ya Allah, he thought as his frown morphed into

a wicked grin. The reason I left without finishing, without taking my pleasure, without satisfying my need is that I wanted to show her that I was in charge, that no matter how aroused I was, I could and would walk away from her if she did not show me the respect I demand as a Sheikh and king. It was a game. It was sport. It was a hunt. That is why I cannot get her out of my mind, yes? Because the game has not been played out. The sport is only just beginning. The hunt is far from over.

All right then, the Sheikh decided, still grinning as he nodded and pulled out his phone and dialed. I showed you that you could not break me, no matter how much I wanted you, no matter how strong my body's need was. Now I will show you that I can break you. I will show you my power. The power of wealth. Let us put my wealth against your principles and see what wins, yes?

"Ibd din allahi," he barked into the phone when one of his assistants back at the Royal Palace of Zahaar answered after one ring. "Her name is Penelope Peterson. She lives in Fargo, North Dakota. Get me her phone number."

# 8

"What?" said Pen, staring out the window as she listened to the voice on the phone. "I don't understand. What did you just say? You want to buy *all* my birds? Why?"

"I will release them into the desert," came the Sheikh's unmistakable voice. "They will live in the shade of the palm trees, cacti, and desert shrubs that grow around the Great Oasis of Zahaar." He paused. "Then I will hunt them."

Pen blinked as she listened to this lunatic say things that barely computed in her frazzled mind. The tingle that had gone through her body when she'd answered the "Blocked ID" call only to hear the Sheikh's voice come through was now a raging current of electricity that had Pen's head buzzing so hard she could barely hear anything. And what she heard sounded like the ramblings of an eccentric madman.

"You're going to release my birds into the desert and then . . . *hunt*them?! In what world does that make any sense at all?!" she managed to say, still blinking as she stared out the window at the white landscape outside. The storm had passed, and although it was well below freezing, the sun was out. It actually looked like a desert out there, with white rolling dunes of pristine snow covering her acreage.

"In the world where I offer you one hundred thousand dollars . . . per bird," replied the Sheikh with a steady nonchalance that made Pen pull the phone away from her ear and then glance at it to make sure she wasn't imagining this conversation.

But the phone's call timer was ticking away, and so Pen took a breath and got back on. "You're offering me what?" she said, her voice so soft she could barely hear herself talk. Or maybe it was the blood pounding in her head when she heard the Sheikh confirm his offer. "You realize I have almost two hundred birds. That would be . . . it would be . . . what, two million dollars?"

"*Twenty* million dollars," said the Sheikh just as Pen calculated it out in her head and almost choked at the number. "And your birds would be free in the wild. They would live in the shade all day, and the desert nights are cool and comfortable. They would be happy."

"But you're going to *hunt* them!" Pen said, trembling as she wondered if she was having a dream. The only thing that confused her was whether this was a fantasy or a goddamn nightmare!

"As man has done for millions of years," came the Sheikh's calm voice. "The birds will have a sporting chance in the wild. A better life than living cooped up in some barn for six months a year, with nothing to excite or amuse them besides their daily feeding."

"And being hunted by some weirdo king with a shotgun is going to excite and amuse them?" Pen shook her head, her eyes widening as she stared out over her white desert. "You're insane," she said blankly. "I knew it when you left, and this only confirms it. Please never call me again."

There was a pause on the other end of the line. Then the Sheikh's voice came through in a hard monotone. "You are turning down twenty million dollars? And *I* am the one who is insane? What is your current source of income, if you do not mind me asking?"

"Um, I *do* mind you asking!"

The Sheikh grunted over the phone. "That answers my question. Your current source of income is nil. Zero. Nothing. You are probably on welfare, supported by your bloated government because of your misguided, childish notion that it is somehow cruel and inhuman to eat animals even though it is as human as it gets. Man has hunted and eaten birds, mammals, reptiles, fish, and goddamn insects since the first ape stood upright and walked the Earth. And—"

"*You're* the goddamn ape!" Pen shouted into the phone, not sure whether she was laughing in amusement or hysteria.

"Ah," said the Sheikh, his calmness driving Pen almost berserk. "Throw some racism in there to top it off, yes?"

"How is that racist?! I'm not calling *all* Arabs apes. I'm just calling *you* an ape!"

"It is not racist towards Arabs," said Rafeez. "It is racist towards apes. Have you ever observed gorillas in the wild? They are peaceful, gentle creatures." He paused, taking a breath, his voice deepening in a way that made Pen weak in the knees, wet between her legs. "And I most certainly am neither peaceful nor gentle."

"That I agree with," Pen said, her eyelids fluttering as she was taken back to the way the Sheikh had taken her . . . or *almost* taken her. Again she was reminded that although he'd seemingly lost control, was about to come inside a woman he'd just met, in the end he'd showed supreme control by stuffing his throbbing cock back in his pants and walking out the damned door! "You're not peaceful. You're not gentle.

And you're not making any sense. I mean, why would you even call me out of the blue and make this ridiculous offer?" She took a breath as she closed her eyes and tried to push away the thought that she already knew the answer to her question. This wasn't about turkeys, just like their first meeting hadn't been about a freakin' turkey! He'd shown up at her doorstep because Willow had sent him there. He'd shown up because for some reason he'd trusted Willow's judgment that the two of them needed to meet. And she'd let him into her house because she'd trusted Willow too.

This was Willow's gift to her. Her last gift as a friend.

What had Willow said the last time they'd hung out? "We need to find you a man. A real man."

So are you going to reject Willow's last gift to you? Or are you going to be grateful and accept it?

Be grateful, Pen thought as she remembered how those words had come to her lips out of the blue at Willow's funeral. Just like the Sheikh had come to her out of the blue. Yeah, he'd disappeared into the blue just as quickly, but now he was back with this outrageous offer to buy her turkeys for twenty million dollars and ship them to the Middle Eastern desert!

Pen took a breath and closed her eyes. Some of what Rafeez had said made a little sense. It couldn't be much fun for her birds to spend the winter living in a barn, with nothing really going on besides their daily feeding. She did her best to keep things clean in there, but there was only so much she could do as one person. Shit. It was probably hellish for those birds all winter!

She'd often considered releasing them into the wild. But where would that end up? Most of them would be killed by foxes, wolves, bears, and the occasional big cat. The rest would be blow to bits by drunk Midwestern "hunters" with machine guns mounted on their pickup trucks. God, she *was* being childish, wasn't she? Naive, stupid, and just plain delusional.

Twenty million dollars, came the thought as she stared at her phone again to make sure it was still on. She couldn't even understand what that kind of money looked like, what it would mean, what it would buy. She could build an animal shelter, name it after Willow, do some real good, have a real impact. She could rebuild this farm, hire good seasonal labor, buy new equipment, grow whatever the hell she wanted. She could even pick up and leave, move to a place where she wouldn't have to dig herself out of a mountain of snow five times a year! Hell, she could move anywhere in the world! She could even move to . . .

Pen blinked as she realized where her thoughts were going, and she felt a catch in her throat as she reminded herself that she didn't know this man, didn't know what kind of game he was playing, whether he was just manipulating her for his amusement, perhaps his massive ego. He was a Sheikh, a king, a man with pride that clearly bordered on arrogance. He was used to dominating everything and everyone in his life, and that was the game unfolding between the two of them. She'd clearly pushed some of his buttons with her comments that day, and maybe no woman had ever talked to him like that before. Maybe he just wanted to . . . win. Dominate her, crush her, and then walk away again. The guy was from a world so far away—both culturally and financially—that Pen couldn't assume she understood anything about him. He might as well be an alien!

What to do, she thought as her mind swirled. What the hell do I do?

"I'll have to see this oasis," she said, almost doubling over in shock when she realized what she was saying. "You say my birds will have a sporting chance out in the wild, that there'll be enough shade for them to survive the days, food for them to live. I'll have to see it for myself. Then I'll decide."

The Sheikh took a breath so loud Pen could hear it over the phone, and she knew his heart had jumped the same way hers had. There's something here, Pen realized as she closed her eyes and saw Willow's smiling face winking at her. Oh God, there's something here.

"Done," came the Sheikh's voice over the phone, breaking Pen out of her daze. "Done."

# 9

**W**hat have I done, thought the Sheikh as he watched his silver jet land at his private airport on the outskirts of Zahaar. The plane had one passenger, and Rafeez's heart pounded as he watched her emerge from the doorway in a scarf and sunglasses, smiling at the attendant who was standing on the tarmac and pointing toward the covered electric cart that would bring her to the terminal. Bring her to him.

Is this just a symptom of unhealthy pride and supreme arrogance, Rafeez wondered as he'd done a hundred times after hanging up the phone with Pen a few days earlier. Is it narcissism? The act of an eccentric king who has lived in a bubble for so long that even the slightest rejection from a woman drives him into a manic frenzy? A woman asks you not to come inside her, and that results in you offering her twenty million dollars and a trip across the world so you can assert your dominance?! Ya Allah, if you open a dictionary and look up the word "insane," will you see your face there?

She was the one who said she needed to see the oasis, Rafeez reminded himself as he took the golden escalator down to the lower level to meet Pen. Which means she understands that this is not about turkeys or even about money. It is about . . .

"Hello!" came her voice, and the Sheikh pushed aside every thought as he felt his mouth widen in a grin at how she was waving like an excited little girl. He could tell she was nervous, perhaps scared out of her mind.

Good, he thought. Because I am scared too. Scared because I do not know if I will be able to turn my back and walk away from her again.

The Sheikh's heart was full as he reached out and squeezed her hand. He wanted to take her in his arms and kiss her hard on the lips, but he held back because of his attendants. Already he knew there would be whispers that would spread about the Sheikh inviting an American woman to the Palace, flying her in on his private jet. He had never hosted a woman at the Palace, holding good to his startling declaration several years earlier that he would never marry, that he was married to his kingdom, his duty, his responsibility to his people and to the future of Zahaar.

"I have decided that I will be the last Sheikh of Zahaar," he'd said in a speech that had sent ripples through the Islamic world and especially the Sheikhdoms of the Arabian Peninsula. "I will not marry. I will not father an heir. And when I pass on to Allah's heaven, the kingdom of Zahaar will become a full-fledged democracy, with leaders elected directly by the people, from the people, *for* the people!"

The announcement had been met with both criticism and praise, with many from the Sheikh's inner circle of ministers begging him to reconsider his move. But Rafeez had been adamant, stating just that democracy was the most reliable system of government, despite its faults.

"No one man should have so much power over so many people," he'd told them. "My father was a decent man and a reasonable Sheikh, but even he had his lapses of judgment, and we have all suffered for it. I do my best to be a benevolent and forward-looking ruler, but there are times when I feel the power of the throne corrupting me. And there is no shortage of examples from the other Sheikhdoms of Arabia where rulers are running their own people and culture into the ground for their own ego, their own gains, even their own pleasures. A ruler must answer to his people, and democracy is the only system of government that ensures that."

Rafeez had declared that when he reached the age of fifty-eight, he would oversee general elections and the transition of power. He would stay on as Sheikh in name as the new government found its feet, but would remain true to his word that he would be the last Sheikh.

"It was a bold move," Charlotte Goodwin had told him when she found a few minutes to speak with him privately at her wedding the previous month. "But what's with the whole 'I will never marry and never father an heir' thing? That seems a bit over the top, don't you think? Hardly necessary."

The Sheikh had smiled thinly, shrugging as he finished his club soda with lime. "My part of the world *is* over the top. Think about what would happen if I married four wives and fathered ten children. What are the chances that after my death, one or more of them would seek to claim the throne, perhaps even seize it in a coup of the democratic leadership that I set up? Then what? A military dictatorship? More of my children fighting over the throne?" He'd shaken his head. "Better to leave no legacy. My legacy will be democracy in Zahaar. Giving a voice to my people. Giving them power over their own lives."

Charlotte had nodded, her blue eyes narrowing as she stood there in her wedding dress. "It's a noble and bold move, like I said. But nothing's going to happen until you're fifty-eight? That's like twenty years away! No wonder people have already stopped talking about it in the news. It seems so far away that I bet people don't believe it's going to happen."

"I do not care. I did not make the declaration to get in the news," Rafeez had said, his jaw stiffening as he realized that he was not being completely honest—not with Charlotte, and not with himself. Certainly he had his pride and his ego, and although he hated to admit it, a part of him cared about being recognized for what he was doing. After all, he was choosing to give up a throne, give up the prospect of marriage, give up the joys of fatherhood!

But in the years that had followed his declaration, Rafeez had not gotten the recognition he thought the announcement warranted. The foreign press had largely ignored it, and even the more liberal news organizations of the Arabian Peninsula had brushed it aside, saying that twenty years was a long time, and who was to say if *any* of the Sheikhdoms would still have kings and queens in twenty years!

Rafeez had sunk into a strange depression during that time, questioning himself and his own motives. A part of him truly believed that this was the right thing to do; another part of him was disappointed that the world did not seem to care; and a third part of him was troubled by the knowledge that he cared so much about what the world thought of him!

The contradictions in his mind and heart twisted him inside out, and finally he'd just said to hell with it and found solace in the one thing he had not sworn off: Sex. Meaningless, raw sex. Why not? He'd only promised to never take a wife and never father a child, yes? He'd never said he was going to become a goddamn monk, letting his balls grow heavy from denying his need, the primal needs of a man.

I am a man, he would tell himself as he visited the private brothels of Dubai and Bahrain, Singapore and Tokyo, Amsterdam and Argentina. A great man. A powerful man. It is no matter if my greatness is not recognized in my time. History will remember me for bringing democracy to the Middle East through peace instead of war, for denying my own needs for the greater needs of the people, the needs of the entire goddamn world.

"*Inshallah*," he would mutter as he rolled on another condom and finished inside another nameless, faceless beauty, his needs getting more manic as time rolled on and the Sheikh felt the clock ticking towards the day he would give up his throne. "God willing I can stay the course, remain true to my word, give up my power when the time comes."

There would be days he questioned his decision, wondering if he had been brainwashed from the years he'd spent in England. Those were the days he'd leave Zahaar in the middle of the night, taking his private jet to Bahrain so he could unleash his frustration on the latest crop of fresh-faced nubiles at his favorite brothel, making them howl in pain and pleasure as he pumped into them from in front and behind, above and below, always hard, always with power, always with a condom. He'd found both solace and satisfaction in these encounters, taking a strange pleasure in knowing that he was denying the primal need of a man to put his seed in a woman. Was that not true strength, real power, the triumph of a man's will over the needs of nature? Of course it was!

But then he'd met Pen Peterson, a goddamn farmgirl from Fargo, North Dakota.

Pen Peterson, the first woman who'd ever felt his bare cock against her inner walls.

Pen Peterson, the only woman who'd actually dared to ask him to pull out when even South American beauty queens and European princesses had begged him to take off his condom and finish inside them.

Pen Peterson, who was now standing before him in all her glory, those curvy hips barely contained by the conservative beige slacks she was wearing, the swell of her breasts calling to him from beneath the long scarf she'd draped around her head and shoulders out of respect for the Arab tradition, her lips full and red . . . and ready.

**10**

"I'm ready," said Pen, doing her best to smile and hold eye contact with the Sheikh even though she could feel her lips trembling, her gaze wavering, her knees shaking. This man did something to her just with his eyes, and with his body in the mix she was a goddamn mess! "Show me the royal hunting grounds where my hundred-thousand dollar birds are going to be gunned down in some lame display of machismo."

The Sheikh raised an eyebrow as his gaze travelled up and down Pen's body. "I see you are still determined on insulting and belittling me. Perhaps I will leave you out in the desert with your beloved birds."

"No problem," said Pen, grinning as she felt the

chemistry she'd felt the first time she'd met the Sheikh . . . before he'd gone all weird on her and disappeared out the front door. "Just don't leave me tied up like the last time, though. That wouldn't be much sport for a manly hunter like yourself."

The Sheikh's green eyes went wide, color rushing to his face, turning his olive complexion dark. Pen almost kicked herself, wondering what the hell she was thinking. But she couldn't help herself. This was who she was, and for some reason she couldn't stop being herself around this man, even though she knew it got under his skin.

Or perhaps that's *why* I can't stop being myself around him, she thought, exhaling when she saw a smile slowly break on his devilishly handsome face.

"You are fortunate none of these attendants speak English," he said sternly, though his tone had an undercurrent of amusement. "Because then I would be forced to have you flogged in the town square for insulting the Sheikh."

"I understand," said Pen, raising her eyebrows in mock innocence and nodding earnestly. "Perception is important, and I'd happily accept the flogging so you can maintain your aura of being an angry God-King."

"God-King! Hah! I like that!" Rafeez laughed, and then he took a breath. "Though in all seriousness, the Sheikh is technically the head of both politics and religion, so in a way the term is accurate."

"Sure," said Pen, adjusting her sunglasses as the Sheikh led her out past the sliding doors of the terminal to where three Range Rovers were parked in a line on the blazing tarmac of the driveway. "Nice chariots, God-King. Which one is ours?"

"Ours? You presume to ride with the God-King himself?"

"Isn't it more presumptuous to think I'll have a gold-plated car all to myself?"

Rafeez laughed as he gestured to an attendant and said something in Arabic. The attendant nodded, bowed, and held open the back doors of the middle car. The Sheikh took a breath, his eyes narrowing as he scanned the bowed heads of all the attendants silently gathered around.

"All right. We will ride together."

Pen frowned when she saw how the Sheikh had glanced at his attendants. "You're worried about what they'll say if we ride together?"

The Sheikh blinked as if she'd seen something he didn't want her to see. "It is no matter. Come. Get in."

Pen dropped the topic and climbed into the golden Range Ranger, feeling a bit self-conscious when she felt her ass stick up in the air as she did it. For a moment the memory of the Sheikh's face between her rear cheeks came to mind, and she felt herself get suddenly wet when she wondered what these attendants would think if they knew that!

Oh, God, what have I gotten myself into by coming here? By *suggesting* that I come here?! This man wanted to come inside me, and when I said no he walked out the door. So what does it mean that I'm back here, of my own free will? Am I saying yes now? Am I saying "Knock me up, God-King?" Am I saying I'm ready to let him finish this meeting the way he wanted to finish that last encounter? Am I submitting just by being here? Does my presence here mean consent? And if so, consent to what? What the hell does this king want from me? Or does he just want . . . me?

Don't be ridiculous, she told herself. It's just a game for him. You have no idea how people like him think. This man grew up amidst fabulous wealth, with an entire nation hailing him as both king and freakin' head-priest or something! Be careful, Pen. Be very, very careful.

Careful, or grateful? thought Pen as she reminded herself why she was here, why she'd even begun down this path in the first place. Friendship, trust, and gratitude. She'd let this stranger into her home simply because Willow had trusted him enough to send him over there. And staying on this path was Pen's way of showing faith in her dead friend, showing gratitude for Willow's last act of friendship.

Besides, she thought with a smile as the tears gathered beneath her sunglasses, Willow would kick my big butt if I turned down a twenty million dollar offer without at least looking into it. So let's just stick with the cover story, shall we? I'm just a turkey farmer here to do due diligence on a proposed business transaction. Perfectly normal, right? Nothing to see here. No weirdo God-King who wants to either knock me up or perhaps tie me to a pillar in the town square and have me flogged. Nope. Everything's normal. Hello!

"Do you not want to freshen up at the Palace before we head to the Great Oasis?" said the Sheikh.

Pen had been lost in her ruminations, and she whipped her head towards him so fast she felt a sudden pain in the back of her neck. "Ow," she muttered, grabbing her neck and rubbing it furiously.

"What is it?" said Rafeez, his face going serious with concern.

"I don't know. I think it's just a catch or cramp or something."

"You are dehydrated and your muscles are cramping. The airplane ride. The dry desert air. It drains your body of moisture and electrolytes." He reached for a sealed bottle of water from the armrest between them. "Here. Drink this. All of it," he commanded.

Pen blinked as the Sheikh cracked open the bottle for her and watched her drink it like she was a child taking her medicine. She finished the last drop and gasped, smiling and blinking as she immediately felt better.

"What is it?" she said. "Doesn't taste like any water I've drunk."

The Sheikh smiled. "It is water from the Great Oasis. Rich in minerals and the Earth's natural salts. Come. Turn for me."

"What?"

The Sheikh didn't answer. Instead he turned her body halfway so she faced the car window. Then he pushed her scarf up and slid his fingers beneath it from behind, making her gasp as his strong fingers touched the bare skin on the back of her neck and shoulders.

"Oh, that feels . . ." she started to say, but the words trailed off when Rafeez's strong fingers dug into her flesh, immediately killing the last of the cramps, sending tingles, sparks, and goddamn flames shooting through her body. "Oh, shit."

Pen heard a mechanical whirring noise, and she fluttered her eyelids open to see a partition rising up between them and the driver. A moment later it was just the Sheikh and her, and suddenly he was pressed close against her as she pushed into him, arching her back and moaning as she felt his lips tease the side of her neck, his breath hot against her skin. His hands slid around her to the front, firmly closing on her breasts and pressing them so hard she cried out as she felt her wetness flow into her panties so quick she wondered if she'd peed herself.

And then he whipped her around, pushing her against the padded door of the moving car, swinging her leg around him so she was spread and breathless before him, staring at the massive peak in his trousers, the need written all over his handsome face.

"I was not going to do this," he grunted, rubbing her mound through her beige slacks, his thumb somehow resting perfectly on her clit, the contact sending a surge of arousal through Pen as she almost choked in shock.

"Oh, really," she managed to say, pushing her hips up involuntarily as her body responded to his touch, every fiber in her calling out "Take me!"

The Sheikh grinned. "No, not really. I was always going to do this. Just perhaps not so soon."

"We can wait until we arrive at the town square if you want," she muttered, taking deep breaths as the Sheikh slowly undid the side zipper of her fitted slacks. He caressed her bare hip as he slowly peeled her slacks off, taking her panties down along with it until she felt the cool leather seat beneath her bare bottom and realized she was naked from the waist down, spread wide in the backseat of a Middle Eastern Sheikh's golden Range Rover as it sped through the desert.

What's happening, she thought, closing her eyes as she smelled herself in the climate-controlled interior of the car. She knew she was wet, dripping all over the smooth white leather interior. But she didn't give a damn. She *couldn't* give a damn—not with the Sheikh's fingers driving through her brown pubic curls, his thumb pressing her clit like a button as he opened her slit wide with the fingers of his other hand.

He brought his face close, licked her twice as if to taste her. Then he smacked his lips and grinned, balancing himself with one knee on the seat and the other foot firmly planted on the floor as he unbuckled and unzipped.

His black silk underwear was so peaked with his erection that Pen couldn't stop staring. She could see a shiny patch of wetness that had oozed through the cloth where his cockhead was pushing against the silk, making it look like a black dome sticking out at the end of a pillar. Then Rafeez pulled the waistband of his underwear down, releasing his cock, and Pen cried out loud when his glistening rod sprung out, gently bouncing as the car raced along the street.

"Oh, shit, that's beautiful," she gushed, turning red when she heard herself speak. She reached out and stroked his glistening shaft with her fingertips, smiling when she saw how his cock flexed at her touch. Oh, God, he wants me so bad, came the thought, and it made her even wetter to see the Sheikh's erection throb as she stroked him. She wanted him too, inside her, all the way inside, filling her, flooding her, fucking her.

He groaned as she stroked him again, his body hardening as his green eyes rolled up in his head.

He let her touch him as he muttered in Arabic, and then he reached for a small compartment near the seat partition and pulled out a condom, tearing the wrapper with his teeth and pushing her hand away from his cock as he rolled it on.

Pen felt a sudden pit in her stomach when she saw Rafeez's magnificent shaft get shielded by the cold, lifeless latex, and she wondered what the hell was wrong with her. This was absolutely the right thing to do, wasn't it? It's what he should have done the first time. It's what she'd *demanded* he do the first time, right? So why was she feeling sick about it? Why was she . . . why was she about to do and say the unthinkable?

"You don't have to," she said, feeling a different sort of sickness rise up in her as she reached for his cock, stroking it again and gently tugging at the bottom of the condom, slowly rolling it up, unsheathing his cock as the Sheikh stared down at her fingers even as he groaned in pleasure at her touch.

"What are you doing?" he said, his voice strained with arousal, his jaw tight, his eyes glazing over as Pen pulled the condom off past the bulb of his cockhead, massaging his massive shaft with one hand as she cupped his balls with the other. "Ya Allah, what are you doing to me?"

Pen had no idea what she was doing. All she knew was that she needed him inside her, and the need was so strong she was almost sickened by it. She'd had a million conversations with Willow about having kids, and while Willow had wanted to be a mother her entire life, Pen had been more-or-less ambivalent about it.

"Maybe the need will kick in at some point," Pen had said when they'd discussed it a few years ago, after Willow and Randy had decided to adopt. Willow had been wondering about whether she'd always regret not carrying her own child, not experiencing that rite of womanhood, of giving birth. Pen had waved it off, saying not every woman had a burning need to get knocked up and go through the pain of labor and delivery, so Willow should just chill and be grateful that they lived in a time and place where a same-sex couple could adopt a child.

"You've never felt that need?" Willow had asked.

"Nope," Pen had replied without hesitation. Then she'd shrugged. "Maybe it'll kick in at some point."

"Yeah, it will. When you get to the end of your Dirty Thirties," Willow had whispered, reaching out and tweaking Pen's nipple, making her scream in surprise.

"Or when the right guy shows up," Pen had said, slapping Willow's hand away and shielding her breasts as the two of them laughed like naughty schoolgirls.

"Yeah, I wouldn't know about that," Willow had replied, rolling her eyes and taking another sip of her drink. Then she'd shrugged. "But all right. I think it's possible that when you see the perfect set of cock and balls—gross, by the way—your pussy will open up like Aladdin's Cave. Open sesame! Put your seed in me! Make me a mommy! Knock me up and turn me into the pregnant bitch I was born to be!"

They'd almost died laughing that night, the two of them getting drunk out of their minds, talking about things that would never be repeated because they were so lewd and gross. Two weeks later Willow and Randy's adoption had come through: Twins from Colombia—a boy and a girl. And then everything had changed. Willow was a mommy without much spare time, and Pen was left behind: just a godmother in her Dirty Thirties . . .

Pen suddenly came back to the present as she heard the Sheikh groan in pleasure once again. She glanced down at herself spread wide, her slit open like Aladdin's Cave, the perfect set of cock and balls at her fingertips, that need to take him into her so strong she could barely breathe. One look at the Sheikh's expression, the way his eyes were rolling up in his head, the way his muscular neck was flexed and thick just like his cock . . . shit, one look at him and she knew he was in her control, at her mercy. He'd come whenever she decided, *wherever* she decided!

She felt a tingle move along her hips, through her buttocks, up along the center of her slit, and in that moment she swore she felt something like static electricity making every strand of hair on her brown triangle stand up straight as it they were opening up a path. She pulled him closer by his balls, which felt heavy and full in her soft hand. A long trail of pre-cum had oozed from the tip of his cockhead and was dripping down onto her mound, the sensation sending ripples through her body. Everything seemed perfect. Even the vibration of the car's engine seemed in tune with their bodies. This was meant to be, wasn't it?

Then for some reason a strange memory flickered into her mind. A memory of the title of an online article she'd seen when she'd looked up Rafeez's name out of curiosity, to see whether he really was a Sheikh. But she'd gotten a phone call related to Willow's funeral arrangements just then, and all that grief had taken her away from the distraction of the Sheikh, making it seem trivial at the time.

Now, however, for some strange reason she could clearly see the headline in her remembered snapshot of the search results:

*Middle Eastern Sheikh Vows to Never Father an Heir.*

She hadn't had a chance to click on the article, and in fact she couldn't be sure the article was even about Rafeez. It was possible his name just happened to be in the text somewhere, which made it show up in the search results. And then with all the madness of Willow's death, Pen had never followed up on it. She hadn't even remembered it until now.

Now or never, came the thought as she heard the Sheikh groan again, saw how his eyes were barely open, how she was pulling him to her, the head of his cock at her opening. He began to push, looking down at her, his tongue darting out as his shaft began its way into her slit, opening her wide as she felt herself getting filled.

Pen was still clutching his balls, and she realized it was the only reason the Sheikh hadn't rammed himself all the way in by now, perhaps pumping his way to orgasm inside her already. He clearly wanted to, and hell, so did she! That was why she was here, wasn't it? Unfinished business? A need so primal it couldn't be denied? And yet she was holding him back from thrusting in all the way, that strange memory mixing with the other strange moments in the little time she'd shared with the Sheikh: That obsession with coming inside her, like it was a deeply forbidden need; the way he'd been startled when she rolled off the condom but yet he let her do it, let her take control of his need, let her . . . decide?

Once again she glanced into his eyes, the memory of her own voice coming back in a whisper. "You don't need that," she'd whispered to him as she ran her fingers along his erection. "Come here. Come in. Come inside me."

No, she suddenly decided. Not like this. I'm not that person. I'm not that woman. God knows my body wants this. Hell, maybe my mind wants it too.

But what about my heart? If I let him do this without knowing the full story, will I be able to live with myself?

Then suddenly Pen pulled on his balls, forcing the Sheikh to draw back. He grunted in surprise, his face twisting in a grimace of momentary anger as the massive head of his cock slid out of her slick vagina, a long trail of pre-cum mixed with her secretions still connecting him to her.

"No," he grunted, trying to push back in. But Pen was firmly in control with her hold on his balls, and he tightened his jaw and looked into her eyes, narrowing his gaze. "I am so close. I need to finish in you. You need it too."

Pen blinked as she tried to hold his piercing eye contact, his narrowed green eyes both angry and surprised at once. Then she shook her head, looking down along her body at his massive brown cock sticking straight out above her smooth, creamy white stomach. "Not like this," she whispered, tears coming to her eyes as she wondered if she was mad, if she was denying her own damned destiny, fighting what felt right in so many ways, overruling her body, her mind, and even the damned King of this land!

And then, without daring to think about it any more, she reached her other hand down, grasped his cock around the shaft, and furiously jerked him back and forth until with a roar he exploded all over her bare belly.

# 11

"Ya Allah!" the Sheikh roared, his body tensing up for a moment and then shattering into a convulsion as she brought him to orgasm with her hand. "No!"

He looked longingly at her slit, and for a moment he almost grabbed her by the throat so she'd release her grip on his balls and let him seed her with the last of his discharge. But the car made a turn just at that moment, and the Sheikh's right hand was pushed against the seat-back so he could keep his balance. Then it was too late, and she was pumping him with all her strength, bringing forth every drop he had, his climax erupting like a volcano, his seed pouring out onto her belly, her chest, her boobs . . . everywhere except where he wanted it to go.

Finally he collapsed on her, his spent cock still

throbbing as it lay flat against her soaked belly. He was panting, he realized. It was one of the strongest orgasms he'd ever had—and it was just from her hand! He was still angry in a way, but he also knew he was smiling. She'd disobeyed him, defied him, damn well *denied* him! Again! Who was this woman?!

Whoever she is, the Sheikh decided in that moment as he lifted his head and looked into her eyes, big brown eyes that seemed to know him even though it was not possible since they had barely spent two hours in the same space . . . yes, whoever she is, I must hold on to her.

"I *will* have you flogged," he mumbled into her hair as he kissed her face and then dropped his head down in exhaustion.

"I think you're the one who just got flogged," she whispered back, her voice sending shivers through the Sheikh, her scent sending sparks through his body, the feel of her body against his making him think of a future that he'd dismissed as impossible: A future with a woman who was actually capable of understanding what he was doing, why he was doing it, and what it would take to support his decision.

"I think I have ruined your scarf," he said, pulling back to look at her and then frowning when he saw that he'd come all over the scarf that was half-undone.

She looked down and nodded. "At least it saved my blouse. Oh, wait. Nope. You got some all over my top too. Wow, that was quite a load. Very impressive."

The Sheikh laughed, slowly separating himself from

her, feeling his cock stick to her belly as he reached for a stack of white silk napkins emblazoned with the seal of the Royal House of Zahaar. He wiped her smooth belly first, then gently dabbed the drops of semen from her matted pubic hair. Already he could feel his cock stir as he touched her, and he saw her stomach move as she gasped. He continued to rub her with the white silk, placing the cloth over her crotch and massaging her through it, his fingers finding her clit and pressing down on the stiff nub.

She came almost immediately, and the Sheikh felt his cock stiffen when he realized how aroused she'd been, how close she'd been, what it must have taken for her to stop him from coming inside her.

You can trust this woman, Rafeez thought as he watched her close her eyes and moan as she came under his touch. He glanced down at the silk square of cloth covering her triangle. It was soaked with her juices, and he pushed his fingers into her cunt, his breath catching as he saw how the shining silk took on the shape of her slit as she shuddered her way through another orgasm.

Yes, you can trust her to make the right decisions. You can trust her to support you, to back up your decisions, strengthen your resolve. She has the heart of a queen, the conscience of a priestess, the mind of a leader. But does she know it? More importantly, does she want it?

She grabbed his hand to stop him, shaking her head as her neck strained with the force of her climax. She moaned so loud the Sheikh was certain the driver would hear even through the soundproof partition, but it no longer mattered. There would already be rumors just from Pen's arrival at the Royal Airport. And so they might as well confirm the rumors, yes?

"Yes?" he said, grinning as he watched her lips tremble. She was still coming, he could tell. Still coming, though he wasn't even touching her anymore. "Yes, my little farmgirl?"

It took almost a full minute for her to open her eyes, and when she did she just smiled and looked up at him. "Firstly, I'm neither little nor a *farmgirl*—whatever the hell that means in your twisted, chauvinistic mind."

The Sheikh took a breath, raising an eyebrow as he let his gaze travel up and down her body. He took in the sight of her pronounced curves, her heavy breasts, her wide hips, solid love-handles that were getting him hard as he pictured flipping her over and holding on as he rammed himself into her from behind. He blinked and shook his head to get the image out of his mind. He knew they would be arriving at the Royal Palace in just a few minutes, and rumors aside, it might be a little disturbing for his staff to catch them naked and wet, their exalted God-King pumping into some American farmgirl's rear.

So Rafeez let out a sigh and shrugged. "All right. I will grant you that. You are not little."

Pen's mouth opened wide with indignation, her eyebrows going up, her brown eyes big and round as she stared up at him. "OK, you just called me fat again! Unbelievable! Get off me, you pig! You body-shaming misogynist!"

The Sheikh groaned and shook his head. "Ya Allah, I should have known it was a trap." He glanced down at his cock, which had filled out again and was gently bouncing with the car's motion. "Clearly my own body is unable to hide its shame. Do you need more proof that I love your body? That I want your body? That I am going to take your body, again and again?"

Pen laughed, slapping at his cock, which only got harder at the contact. "*Take* my body? You sound like an alien. But all right. Clearly your Neanderthal hind-brain is drawn to my womanly curves, so I'll let you off the hook. But *farmgirl*? What's that about?"

"Are you not a farmgirl?" said Rafeez, raising the other eyebrow.

"Are you not a misogynistic ape who fetishizes Western women?" said Pen, raising both eyebrows.

"I fetishize all women equally."

Pen laughed. "Well, that's much better. An equal opportunity ape."

The Sheikh grunted. "You know that calling me an ape is racist. Degrading. Politically incorrect."

"Oh, I call every man an ape," said Pen innocently. "It's got nothing to do with the color of your skin."

"It must be my gorilla-sized cock," grunted the Sheikh, glancing up through the tinted windows and sighing. "Which I must now squeeze back into my trousers since we will be pulling up to the front entrance of the Royal Palace."

"Oh, shit!" said Pen, color rushing to her face as she sat up and frantically reached for her slacks. "I can't let anyone see me like this! They're gonna think I'm some whore!"

"Do not worry," said the Sheikh, grinning wide as he grabbed her slacks and held them away from her as she tried to claw her way across his massive body to get at them. "I will tell them you are an American farmgirl who does not wear pants or panties. I will explain that in the free land of America, farmgirls roam the fields naked from the waist down, with bushels of corn propped against their wide hips, their virginal pussies dripping with the nectar of democracy and capitalism."

Pen almost choked with laughter, her eyes going wide as she finally got a hold of her slacks and yanked them from the Sheikh. "You should be a poet," she remarked, still giggling as she pulled her slacks on without bothering to search for her underwear. "You'd win the Nobel Prize for imagery like that."

"Right now the only image in my mind is that of your virginal pussy dripping with—"

"OK, stop!" Pen said, slapping his hands away as the Sheikh reached for her crotch just as she managed to pull her slacks up past her hips. "You're sick! And who uses the word *virginal* in a sentence these days?"

"An Arabian God-King who is also a poet may use any words he chooses," said Rafeez, finally pulling his hands away and letting Pen zip up just as the car pulled to a smooth stop and the door slowly opened as if by magic "Ibd din allahi," he said to the silent attendant holding the door open for them. "Other side first, please. The lady alights before the Sheikh."

**12**

Am I a lady now, Pen wondered as she realized her shoes had come off in the car. Does a lady bend over and grope around beneath the seat to find her shoes?

Nope, she decided as the attendant's gaze momentarily shifted to Pen's eyes before he quickly bowed his head and stepped back after making sure the door stayed open. Then he hurried around to the other side of the car and pulled open the Sheikh's door.

"Thank you," said Pen, smiling and waving toward the attendant, who broke into a huge, toothy grin that indicated Sheikh Rafeez's staff had excellent dental coverage.

"Ibd din allahi," she heard the Sheikh say as she

kicked around beneath the seat with her bare foot, doing her best to find those damned shoes.

Suddenly the attendant was back, and somehow he was reaching beneath the seat in front of her, his thin arms making their way deep down and coming back out with her shoes. His grin grew wider as he placed the shoes on the marbled portion of the driveway where they'd stopped, and Pen shrugged and stepped into them, feeling like Cinderella for a moment.

But not the Cinderella who spent her days in the pantry, it occurred to her as she glanced up and gasped at the splendor of the Royal Palace of Zahaar, its motif done in white marble, pristine like snow, shining like a jewel in the desert sun. The enormously thick pillars lining the front entrance were too numerous to count, seemingly stretching to infinity on either side of her as she stood there dumbstruck, gaping like a goldfish plucked from its bowl.

Or maybe I've stepped into the bowl. Or into the bubble. Either way, this can't be real. This can't be happening. Not to me. Could it?

Again she thought of Willow, and immediately her heart filled with that strange sense of gratitude, of thankfulness, of pure and simple love for a friend.

"Thank you for putting me here, Willow," she whispered as she looked up and saw two towering minarets marking the front corners of the Royal Palace. They seemed to reach up into the clear blue sky, white marble shining so bright it made her head spin. Each minaret was topped with a peak done in shimmering gold paint. Or at least it looked like gold paint. It was probably a bit crude to ask if the Sheikh's minarets were plated with real gold.

Pen pulled her scarf tighter around her head and neck as she waited there alone, feeling somewhat awkward as she heard the Sheikh saying something to another attendant behind her. She took a breath, her knees going weak when she caught the aroma of the Sheikh's semen and she remembered that hell, she was covered in it. Talk about crude!

She tried to feel dirty, ashamed, embarrassed, but her heart was still full of gratitude and wonder. And when she turned halfway and saw that the Sheikh had sent his attendants away and was now just standing there alone, gazing at her with a faraway look in his green eyes that were somehow still focused on her, she smiled and closed her eyes so she could bask in this moment.

There's so much potential in this moment, she thought. Here I am, standing at the front entrance of an Arabian Palace, a God-King staring at me with what looks like desire in his eyes—maybe more. And it's all because Willow put me and him in the same room. What a parting gift! I need to make sure I don't squander it, like I almost did when I pretty much chased him off my farm two weeks ago!

"Are you done staring at my humble home like you have never seen a Royal Palace before?" came his voice through her thoughts, and Pen gasped when she felt his strong arm circling her waist, smelled his masculine scent rise up to her through his white linen shirt.

"What about perception? Rumors? Palace gossip?" she asked, shifting closer to him almost involuntarily, like it was natural, like it was right.

"I told you, it is too late to stop that, so we might as well confirm it."

"Confirm what?" Pen said, immediately blushing when she realized that the question was premature, that they'd technically not even had sex yet. If anything, this was just the second date. Too early for her to ask, "Where is this going?!" like some psycho chick.

"That you and I will be married," said the Sheikh, his tone barely changing as he said the words. "Come. Let me show you your new home."

Pen's knees almost gave way as she let the Sheikh lead her up the majestic marble steps that rose up like a pyramid. She knew she was hearing things, that he couldn't have said what he'd just said. Of course not. It was sun madness. Heat stroke. Desert insanity. Whatever.

"My new . . . what?"

The Sheikh half-turned, one eyebrow raised, his green eyes calmly focusing on her face. "Home. A husband and wife typically live in the same home. Is that not how it works in your curious American farm-girl culture?" He glanced up at the massive teakwood double doors, the dark old wood polished smooth, the frame inset with Arabic inscriptions scripted in gold, studded with precious stones of every color imaginable. "Of course, when the husband and wife are also a king and queen, the home is a Royal Palace. Come. Do not trip on the stairs. Come."

Pen blinked as she stumbled, grabbing onto the Sheikh's strong arm, which felt stable as one of those massive pillars. Indeed, everything about Rafeez seemed calm and stable right then, a cool confidence oozing out of him, his green eyes focused in a way that sent chills up and down her spine. This man had made a decision, she realized as she gasped for air, trying desperately to push back the thoughts that threatened to drown her. Who makes a decision like that?!

A king does, she realized as she clutched Rafeez's arms tighter and took the last few steps with all the grace she could muster under the circumstances. A tremble went through her as those double doors opened like magic, revealing a courtyard with black marble fountains and palm trees, gazebos made of polished teakwood, pathways of red sandstone, attendants in white robes standing silently at the edges of the courtyard, heads bowed to acknowledge the return of their Sheikh.

He is a God-King, isn't he, Pen thought as she surveyed the perfect proportions of everything in the courtyard, how the open hallways lining the borders were geometrically aligned to give the whole scene a dazzling yet tranquil effect. The way the attendants were lined up seemed staged but yet natural, like petals on a flower.

Again Pen smelled his semen on her clothes and skin, and her head spun as she began to hyperventilate. It was too much. Just too fucking much. The way the Sheikh had stormed into her life in the middle of a snowstorm before walking out the door, leaving her tied to her own dining table like a piece of leftover meat. Then Willow's sudden death followed by this madman nonchalantly offering her twenty million dollars to buy her turkeys so he could seed his private hunting ground.

An offer which you didn't turn down, by the way, Pen reminded herself when she realized she wasn't going to faint after all. Perhaps you *should* have turned it down, just to keep this weirdo out of your life. But no, you came up with the ludicrous suggestion to actually come and see this Great Oasis where your turkeys will run free like God's creatures were meant to, hunted by Arabs on camels or whatever.

Oh God, she thought as she remembered that this wasn't about turkeys, that it was never about turkeys, that she was the goddamn turkey if she thought it was about turkeys! This entire thing *was* a marriage proposal, wasn't it? The phone call. The question. And my response. Sure, we were talking about some ridiculous offer to buy a flock of flightless birds, but really we were talking about us, about this, about . . .

"Trust," said the Sheikh, turning to her as they stood in the center of the perfectly proportioned courtyard. "We were brought together because each of us trusted your friend. We are standing here together because each of us trusted our instincts, our need to be close to one another regardless of the superficial details of how long we have known each other."

"Yes, but . . . but . . . *marriage*?!" Pen stammered, blinking as she felt that sickness rise up again, that feeling like she was Cinderella and it was three strokes to midnight and she was about to turn back into a pumpkin—or whatever the hell happened to Cinderella at midnight after the magic wore off and the fantasy faded.

"What is marriage if not an exercise in trust?" said Rafeez. "I have always trusted my instincts, trusted my body, trusted my nature. That is why when I decided I would never father an heir, I knew I would also need to commit to never being married. I understood that my needs are so strong that there would be times when my resolve would weaken, when the forces of nature, the urges of the body would take over. And I never believed I would find a woman whom I could trust to stop me when that happened. Not until I met you."

Pen blinked in disbelief as she listened. She looked down, glancing at her feet. She remembered reading somewhere that if you're trying to figure out whether you're in a dream, you should look at your feet. If you're dreaming, you won't be able to see your feet.

Well, I have feet in this dream, Pen thought, but it's clearly still a dream. A dream where a fat-assed farmgirl from Fargo meets an Arabian Sheikh who wants to knock her up. But she refuses because . . . "reasons" . . . and she refuses again because . . . "morals" . . . and now the Sheikh wants to marry her because he believes he can trust her to always refuse when his need to knock her up gets so strong that he can't trust himself to stop. You couldn't make this shit up, and if you did, it would be one of those *Mills and Boon* comic books.

"I think maybe it's time I freshened up," Pen said weakly, forcing a smile as she felt her head spin again. "I just need . . . I need a minute."

## 13

**I** need a minute as well, thought the Sheikh as he watched one of his female attendants lead Pen towards the Eastern Wing of the Royal Palace. He blinked as he tried not to stare at her buttocks move in those beige pants, but he could not keep his eyes off her. He could barely keep his hands off her, and Rafeez wondered if the years of denying himself a normal relationship with a woman had twisted him into a caricature, his personality and character just a comical mix of a schoolboy's lust and a megalomaniac's ego.

He'd arrived at the decision to marry her suddenly, naturally, implicitly. There had been no internal debate, no real thought process behind it. The moment he stepped out of the car and stood by her side he knew she was his partner, his wife, his queen, his Sheikha. She was his, and that was all there was to it.

It is like an arranged marriage of old, Rafeez thought as he began to pace the crisscrossed pathways of the courtyard, the same pathways he'd run through as the only living child of parents who'd had him late in life. There'd been an older sister who'd died before her time, and then no children until little Rafeez arrived. He'd been coddled and spoiled, treated as if he were a miracle baby, a gift from Allah. His father the old Sheikh had taken three wives in his lifetime, but only one of them had borne him that coveted son—and that too when she was in her late forties: a miracle indeed.

The old Sheikh himself had been in his sixties when Rafeez was born, and it was only much later that Rafeez seriously wondered what his father was planning for the kingdom's future if his only heir had showed up unexpectedly in the old Sheikh's twilight years. And Rafeez found his answer one evening while combing through some old documents in his father's private library in the North Wing of the Royal Palace, a room so messy and unkempt that Rafeez wondered how in the world his father had managed to run a kingdom!

The document was an edict, a directive issued directly by the Sheikh. Of course, it was still in draft form, never issued, never published, never made public. Because the arrival of little Rafeez, the miracle baby, Allah's surprise gift had apparently changed the Sheikh's mind:

*The time of kings and queens, Sheikhs and Sheikhas, crowns and scepters is gone. This is the age of democracy and individualism, where the common man has earned the right to make his choices, pursue his dreams, claim his destiny. And so I hereby declare I will be the last Sheikh of Zahaar. Allah has decreed it by denying my three wives a son, denying our kingdom an heir. So be it. The message is clear, and I will accept it. Inshallah. Allah hu Akbar.*

The rest of the document went on to describe the peaceful transition to democracy, the establishment of a President and Cabinet of Ministers, the set up of elections for members of legislatures and houses of congress. It was well thought out, and it had affected young Rafeez deeply—especially during the three years he spent in England, studying at Oxford University, mingling with an eclectic group ranging from the entitled children of the world's leftover royal families to some of the same world's most brilliant "commoners," those who'd earned a spot through their own merits and hard work.

My arrival destroyed my father's dreams for our kingdom, he'd finally decided when he returned to Zahaar and took back active control of his kingdom's affairs. His council of ministers had adequately managed things while Rafeez was in England, just like they'd managed things well enough while he was a teenager still learning how to be a king. Clearly the nation could function under the guidance of a similar group of ministers and leaders, Rafeez realized. And perhaps it should. Perhaps my father was right. Perhaps my arrival was not a gift from Allah but simply a test of my father's resolve, to see if he could put aside pride, ego, and nepotism to lead his nation into the new world of democracy and individual freedom!

And so perhaps the burden now falls upon me, the son. Perhaps now I need to prove that I can overcome my ego, my selfishness, my pride. Do what my father failed to do: Choose the future of my kingdom over the selfish need to see my own heir sit upon the throne.

At first Rafeez had decided it would be simple enough to transition Zahaar to democracy while raising a family of his own. There was no need to deny himself the basic needs of a man, was there? But then he'd watched several smaller Sheikhdoms descend into civil war after their Sheikh had died without naming a successor. Sons and daughters plotted against one another. Cousins and distant relatives formed alliances, raised small armies, planned assassinations. No, he'd decided. Our bloodline is clear and our family tree has very few branches. If I do not have children, there would be no one with a reasonable claim to the throne. All I have to do is make that one sacrifice, and I will go down in history as the Father of Democracy in Zahaar! Is that not a legacy I can be proud of?!

And so Rafeez had issued his announcement, committing to never fathering an heir, never satisfying his animalistic need to spread his seed. He'd also decided it meant he could never marry, because what woman would be satisfied with being denied a child by rule? Even if he found a woman who agreed, how could he trust her to keep her word when it went against everything both their bodies demanded? There was no woman he could trust to that extent.

Except perhaps the woman who'd just walked through his courtyard in beige slacks, thought Rafeez as he rubbed his jawline and grinned, shaking his head as he reminded himself that he'd just told her they would be married. He hadn't asked. He hadn't offered. There was no proposal. He'd just said it like it was done. Case closed.

"Case closed," the Sheikh said out loud as he paced, trying to ignore the tension rising along his back, the excitement making his body tingle, the anticipation making him clench his fists. Suddenly he felt vulnerable, an uncharacteristic panic whipping through him as he wondered what he might do if she emerged shaking her head, telling him he was insane, that she couldn't possibly go along with what he'd decided, that she would never in a million years marry him!

And then the Sheikh knew he was smitten, trapped, defeated. She'd gotten under his skin, and she had a hold on him whether she knew it or not. For a moment he thought back to that short-haired friend who'd spoken to him at Charlotte's wedding and arranged the meeting with Pen.

"Thank you," he whispered, clenching his fists again and grinning at the way the blood pounded in his temples as he awaited Pen's decision on his decision. "Thank you for sending her to me. I will find a way to repay you, to express my gratitude for your gift."

But first I need to seal the deal with this curvy farmgirl, he thought as he stopped near the edge of one of the black marble fountains in the open courtyard, glancing down into his own reflection. Close the case.

## 14

**P**en closed her make-up case and smiled at herself in the mirror. Then she frowned and puffed out her cheeks. This is a fat mirror, she decided as she took a few steps back and put her hands on her hips, turning sideways and sucking in her belly.

"Mirror mirror on the wall," she whispered, facing the wood-framed oval glass and smiling as she felt a strange tingle move along her buttocks and up her spine, "who's the fattest farmgirl of them all?"

"You are," she replied, giggling as she shook her head at the madness of it all. "You are!"

All right, she told herself. You have to go out there and face him. Tell him that you're flattered by his offer, but you can't possibly accept it. Hell, you don't even know him! And from what you do know, he's erratic, entitled, arrogant, and possibly insane!

He's also smoking hot, a billionaire king, and he clearly can't keep his hands off you, another part of her whispered as she exhaled hard and frowned at herself in the mirror. Besides, Willow believed in him from one meeting! When has she ever set you up with a guy? Never! You already pushed him out of your life once, refused Willow's gift. And then he came back, and so did you! You're here, with him, in a Royal Palace that he just said was going to be your new home! Don't be a moron, Pen! Just do it! Don't look a gift-horse in the mouth!

He doesn't want children, which means that if it doesn't work, it won't get too complicated to split up, Pen reasoned as she felt that chill spread out through her body until she was a quivering mess. So think of it like an arranged marriage or something. You've already been pretty damned intimate with him. And yeah, he's been kinda weird, taken things to places you've never imagined going before. But hell, now you're imagining going to those places with him, aren't you? So maybe you should just do it! See what happens!

And so before she could second-guess herself, Pen took a breath and walked back out into the courtyard where the Sheikh was standing near a black marble fountain. She could see the tension on his handsome brown face, and it somehow excited her to know that this was important to him, that although he'd made the statement with authority and resolve, like it was a decision that couldn't be challenged, it was clear that it was also a question. It was indeed a proposal. In his own way, the Sheikh was asking, "Will you marry me?"

Pen blinked as she wondered what to say. And then the words came. Her answer came.

"What about my birds?" she blurted out. "Will you still hunt them like some savage?"

The Sheikh frowned, and then he burst into a smile as if he'd just remembered that none of this was about the damned turkeys. He shrugged, raising his chin and narrowing his eyes as he came close. "The birds will be given their freedom. Then they can take their own chances. It is the way of nature."

Pen felt herself smile as she realized they were speaking in metaphors, with her turkeys just a proxy for their relationship, for how things would play out. "No children," she said slowly. "And my birds are going to live in some Arabian oasis-paradise with nothing to fear except the occasional hunting mission from a mad shotgun-wielding Sheikh on a camel."

"That seems like a classic set of conditions for a conventional arranged marriage," said Rafeez, slowly walking towards her, his face comically serious. "Though my weapon of choice is up for debate."

"Oh, really?" said Pen, glancing at his crotch, gasping when she saw it was obscenely filled out, pushing the front of his trousers up into a peak that rivaled the minarets of the Royal Palace. "I don't think there's any debate as to your weapon of choice, Your Highness."

"So that is a yes?" said the Sheikh, stepping up so close she could smell his natural scent, an aroma that felt familiar now, felt like home. "Not that it was a question," he added hurriedly.

"Of course not," Pen said, blinking when she realized it wasn't clear what she was talking about. "I mean, of course it wasn't a question. And yeah, the answer is yes. Sure. What the hell. Let's get married. What's the worst that can happen?"

## 15

"Wait, *what* just happened?" Pen said, pulling the phone away from her ear and glancing at it. It seemed like she'd been doing a lot of that lately. Why was her iPhone showing up in so many crazy dreams? "No, that's impossible. There must be some mistake."

"I'm sorry, Ms. Peterson," came the solemn voice on the other end. "There's no mistake. She was found this morning. She drowned in her bathtub. I'm sorry, Ms. Peterson."

Pen just blinked as she listened to the female police officer tell her that Randy, Willow's partner, had been found dead that morning, drowned in her own bathtub. "OK . . ." she said, blinking again and making eye contact with the Sheikh, who was frowning with concern as he looked at her from across the dinner table. Zahaar was nine hours ahead of the United States, and so it was just past sunset their time, ten in the morning in Fargo.

Pen nodded through the rest of the phone call, unable to speak. Her mind was alternating between going completely blank and running a mile a minute, and by the time she hung up and sat down in the high-backed teakwood chair, her heart was beating so fast she thought she was going to die.

"Randy's dead," she said, her voice deadpan, her expression stoic, her head still spinning.

"Who is Randy?" said the Sheikh.

"Willow's partner," said Pen, realizing that she and the Sheikh still knew so little about one another's lives. Hell, they'd groaned and moaned together longer than they'd actually talked! What the hell was she doing marrying this guy!

Well, that's not gonna last long, she reminded herself as she thought a few steps ahead and swallowed hard as a chill descended on her, cold and dark like a North Dakota winter.

"I am sorry to hear that. That was Willow on the phone?" the Sheikh continued, dabbing his mouth with a black silk napkin and leaning back, giving her his full attention in a way that made Pen's heart leap just a teeny bit.

Pen frowned, and then her eyes widened when she realized that shit, he didn't even know that Willow was dead! "Uh, no," she said slowly. "Willow was killed in a car accident a few weeks ago. I thought I told you that."

The Sheikh's expression changed so fast it startled Pen, and it was only when she saw him swallow hard and clench his jaw that she realized Willow meant something to him, that even the seemingly insignificant meeting had been meaningful to the Sheikh. "You did not," he said slowly, glancing down at his hands and muttering something in Arabic under his breath. Then he looked up, his expression back to normal. "I am sad to hear that. She was a good person. A good friend." He paused again, offering a smile. "And a very good matchmaker."

Pen couldn't help smiling back, and when the Sheikh reached out his hand she nodded and came over to him. He pulled her down onto his lap, kissing her hair, her forehead, her cheeks, holding her close as he did it.

This feels good, Pen thought as she felt the Sheikh take her weight easily. She leaned against his strong, hard, massive body, her own body suddenly alive with waves of warmth, sparks of heat, feelings of . . . love?

"Was Randy's death a suicide?" he asked finally, caressing her hair gently.

Pen shook her head. "The police said it was an accident, far as they can tell. They're still doing an autopsy to see if there were drugs in her system, but for now they're saying it was just an accident."

"The police? Why were they calling you? Are you the next of kin for Randy? Her emergency contact?"

"Hah! No," said Pen, rolling her eyes. "Randy didn't like me much. And she's got parents—though her parents pretty much disowned her after she came out and married Willow. Still, I'm sure the cops called Randy's parents before they called me."

"But why call you at all? Do the American police call everyone in someone's phonebook when they are found dead?"

Pen shifted on the Sheikh's lap, and suddenly that warmth was chased away by the fear of what she was about to tell him. And then she realized it was something she should have told him before she'd agreed to marry him, and the fear escalated so fast Pen thought she was choking.

Slowly she moved off Rafeez, taking a breath as she stepped away from him, her face towards the floor-to-ceiling windows that overlooked the dark dunes of the Zahaari Desert.

"Because I'm the godmother of Randy and Willow's children," she said quietly, the gravity of it hitting her only as she said the words. Her knees almost buckled as she turned back to the Sheikh, and she gulped back her fear and looked him right in the eyes as she felt her future melting away, the palace crumbling into dust, leaving nothing but Pen and two adopted babies. "And that means those kids are mine now, Rafeez. Those kids are mine!"

The silence was so heavy in that old dining room that Pen swore it was crushing them, crushing the Palace itself. The only condition he'd put upon their marriage was that they'd never have children, and now, one day after she'd said yes, she was basically telling him she was also a single mom with twins!

Oh, God, my marriage is over before it even started, came the thought as her heart beat so hard she thought it would explode right then, darting right out of her chest and bouncing merrily around the floor, laughing at her for being naive enough to think this was actually gonna happen in the first place! Married to a king? Sure, honey. Dream another dream, you fat-assed floozy—'cause this dream is over. Done. Finished.

"Well, at least it'll be a great story to tell the kids when they're older," Pen whispered as she turned away from the Sheikh, not bearing to see the disappointment on his face. "Mommy was engaged to an Arabian King once, you know. A Sheikh! We were engaged for one day, and then you two came into my life and the Sheikh walked out of it. But it's OK. I promised Willow I'd be there if anything ever happened to her and her partner. Of course, I never imagined

I'd actually have to make good on that promise. Who the hell expects both parents to die within a month of each other, in separate accidents! What are the fucking chances?!"

"Are you talking to me or yourself?" came the Sheikh's deep voice from behind her, and Pen almost jumped as she was pulled back to the moment.

Still, she couldn't turn to face him. She couldn't face what she knew was coming. And then suddenly she hated Willow, hated Randy, even hated those innocent kids who'd already lost two sets of parents. And then she hated herself for having those thoughts, for being so selfish that she resented everyone else for taking away her future, her dream, her happily-ever-after. Who the hell was she gonna find now, saddled with twins from Colombia of all places! She was going to grow old as a single mom, working on a goddamn turkey farm, trying to get people to make turkey-egg omelets so she wouldn't have to slaughter those dumb, fat-assed birds!

Fuck it, she suddenly thought. Fuck it all.

Then she turned and looked up at the Sheikh. "Our deal with the turkeys still good? Twenty million for the bunch?"

Rafeez blinked as he stared into Pen's eyes. For a moment she thought he was going to break into a smile, wave away her fears, pull her into his massive body and kiss her forehead like he'd just done. She thought he was going to say everything would be all right, that they would work it out, find a compromise, that her children were his children now. That was what a man did, right?

At least that was what a man in love would do . . .

The Sheikh opened his mouth as if to say something, but then his jaw went tight, his eyes narrowed, and he nodded his head. "Our deal is still good. I will arrange for the transport, and as agreed, they will be released into the wild." He paused for a moment, rubbing his heavy stubble. "You understand that what I said about hunting them still holds," he whispered, the words coming slowly, almost like he was issuing a challenge, giving her another chance to back out, perhaps to beg him for some compromise. "I make no guarantees for their safety."

"Kill 'em all," said Pen as she felt a dark cloud descend over her even as the pit in her stomach grew so heavy she thought it would drag her right through the sandstone floor. "Kill 'em all, for all I care."

And then she walked right past the Sheikh, almost bursting into tears as she took one last breath of his scent, holding it in because she knew she'd never smell it again. It was over. It had lasted one day, and now it was over. Sure, this had never been about those damned turkeys, but now Pen realized it had never been about her and the Sheikh either. Both she and the Sheikh were committed to something bigger, and they were being called to make sacrifices for their larger goals. The Sheikh had to choose his country over his marriage. And Pen had to choose the children over the Sheikh.

There's no choice to make, Pen told herself as she realized she was still hoping Rafeez would run across the room and gather her into his arms like in a movie or something.

But then she was at the door, and the Sheikh was still at the far end of the room, standing still as a statue, his green eyes narrowed as he watched her leave . . .

. . . as he let her leave.

# 16

**Y**ou let her leave. How could you let her leave?!

The Sheikh watched as his men unloaded crate after crate of squawking turkeys from the belly of the freight airplane he'd sent to Fargo. He'd made good on his offer, even though the offer had been about the woman, not the bloody birds. What in Allah's name was he going to do with two hundred American turkeys? Would they even survive in the desert heat? Would he have to build an air-conditioned biodome for them? Would his people finally decide their Sheikh had lost touch with reality once they were chased and pecked by turkeys while on family picnics at the Great Oasis?

Perhaps this will accelerate the move to democracy and the end of the Royal Line of Zahaar, the Sheikh thought as he tried to push away that last image of his American farmgirl, her wide hips swinging as she defiantly walked past him and out the door, out of his life.

And you let her walk away, Rafeez thought again, closing his eyes and clenching his fists. But what else could you do? You could not commit to taking on two adopted children, and at the same time, you could not ask her to turn her back on her own commitment as godmother! What a mess! Ya Allah, what a bloody mess!

The Sheikh ran his fingers through his thick black hair, pulling hard at the roots until he felt the sharp clarity of pain spreading across his scalp. It felt good, the pain. It distracted him from the pain in his heart, a pain he didn't understand—or rather, didn't *want* to understand.

Is that what love feels like, he wondered as he watched the last of the turkeys get unloaded, one of the big birds cocking its head and looking him dead on in the eye as if to tell him he was a fool for letting her walk out of his life. Pain, anguish, loss? Is that the price I must pay for the decisions I've made, the decisions my father made but never followed through with?

And then the Sheikh hated his father, hated the

old man for putting him in this position. If the old Sheikh had simply followed through on his decision, then Rafeez would be just a normal billionaire in the Democratic Republic of Zahaar. But no, the old man had weakened at the sight of his giggling baby boy, and he'd decided to hand the child his kingdom, his throne, and the responsibility to make up for the sins of the father.

What now, thought Rafeez, clenching his fists tighter as the squawking threatened to drive him insane. Ya Allah, what now?!

And then it hit him, and he broke into a grin, the smile spreading across his entire face, perhaps his entire body. It was so simple. Why not? Why the hell not?

Yes, I will do it, Rafeez decided. But not yet. I must give it some time, just so I am certain the decision is not being made in haste. Three months. I will give it three months, and if I still feel this way, I will go to her.

# 17
# **THREE MONTHS LATER**

**T**he twins were dressed and ready for school by eight, and Pen loaded them into the backseat of her black Range Rover and strapped them in nice and tight. She paused for a moment before getting into the driver's seat, scanning her farm's acreage and sighing. Spring was almost here, and the new greenhouses had been built to perfection. Soon she'd be growing organic kale and hydroponic tomatoes all year round, all of it in a controlled environment funded by the Sheikh's outrageous deal.

It was all funded by the Sheikh, she realized as she

ran her finger along the top of her shiny new Range Rover, looked up at the refurbished (and refurnished) farmhouse that was as close to a mansion as you could get within the limitations of the current architecture. The twins' future was secure: They'd never have to worry about paying for college or pursuing whatever dreams they had. As for her . . . she was living a dream too, wasn't she?

But a wave of melancholy swept over her as she got into her car and glanced at the twins in the rearview mirror, their sweet brown faces shining like the sun. They'd been sad and scared after losing their two American moms, but they'd bounced back like resilient young kids. They were fine. They would be fine.

But what about you—are *you* fine? Pen thought, that melancholy twisting inside her until she had to close her eyes and push away the image of the Sheikh, of what might have been, of what *she* might have been! A queen? A princess? A Sheikha riding camels through the desert with her Sheikh leading her? Who knows what experiences she'd have had! And now she was resigned to raising someone else's kids, rich but alone, secure but broken, forever doomed to live in the shadow of what might have been.

"Be grateful," she whispered, closing her eyes tight and then opening them, relieved that the tears hadn't flowed down her round cheeks, like they had so often over the past three months. "You're still getting to do something very few others get to do: Be a mother to two wonderful children. Make good on a promise to a dear friend. And you're fucking rich. So get over yourself, you fat cow! Think of the children starving in Africa or Guatemala or wherever they're starving these days and be grateful for what you have. Be *grateful*!"

Besides, she thought as she tightened her jaw and started up the car's engine, you barely knew the Sheikh. Don't build it up into something that's gonna make you pine for him the rest of your life. Who's to say you'd even be together now. Who's to say he wouldn't have backed out of the wedding anyway. It was a ridiculous idea to begin with! Who decides to get married after meeting twice?!

Just every royal couple in the history of every great culture, came the answer from an annoyingly pedantic part of Pen's brain—the part that had wistfully read up on the long history of arranged marriages in cultures ranging from the medieval French and English to modern-day India. There were even arranged marriages taking places in secret in the elite levels of American society—which was as close to royalty as you could get in the good ol' U.S. of A!

That melancholy was still weighing her down as she pulled up at the driveway to the private school where the twins had just started that past Fall. She kept the engine running as she unstrapped the kids and took them into the building, kissing them each on the forehead and saying bye with a big smile, feeling like a fraud as she did it even though she knew she loved them.

Yes, of course I love them, she told herself, that pit in her stomach feeling like a rock that was choking her, dragging her to the ground, making each step she took feel heavy with guilt. Again she thought of Willow and how she'd agreed to be Godmother to the twins. She hadn't thought about it much at the time: Hell, what Godmother actually expects to be called upon to make good on her promise?!

Stop it, she told herself, almost saying it out loud as she emerged from the school building so fast she almost knocked over a train of six-year-olds holding hands, led by a teacher. The teacher glared at Pen, looking her up and down, her gaze resting on her cleavage for a moment before meeting her eyes. Pen could see the disapproval in the teacher's expression, and she almost laughed as she wondered how it was that she'd turned out to be a horrible person: a wealthy single mom who wore low cut dresses to drop her kids off at school while dreaming of being with some alpha bad-boy who didn't want kids at all . . .

Pen was so lost in her thoughts that at first she didn't notice the tall, lithe figure leaning against the gently humming hood of her Range Rover. And when she did, she frowned and sighed.

"All right, all right," Pen said, slightly irritated but

mostly at herself for being an ungrateful wretch of a woman for having such horrible thoughts, "I'll move the car in a minute. What's the rush? There's no one else in the driveway!"

"Do I look like the traffic police?" said the woman, adjusting her sunglasses and smiling, her red lips parting to reveal perfectly aligned white teeth that had almost certainly been professionally polished that week. Perhaps every week.

Pen ran her tongue between her lips and teeth, blinking as she stared up at the tall, thin blonde leaning against her Range Rover like she owned it. Shit, I need to get my teeth straightened, Pen thought absentmindedly as she smiled without showing her own teeth to this supermodel.

"What is this, PTA recruitment?" Pen said, raising an eyebrow and reaching for her door handle. She hadn't interacted much with the other parents yet, and this wasn't the time. She was still too turned around with everything that had happened over the past few months. Everything was still too new. New money. New kids. New life. And that nagging feeling like everything was about to go to shit. Or that perhaps it already *had* gone to shit!

The woman laughed, taking off her sunglasses and tossing back her long, flowing blonde hair like this was a shampoo commercial. "That's funny! Oh, you're so cute," she said, touching Pen's shoulder in a way that made Pen want to punch this condescending wench in the mouth and say something like, "Do you know who I am? I'm a millionaire! And I was engaged to a Sheikh once! Cute? Funny? Let's see what you think when I break your porcelain nose, you Barbie-doll *bitch*!"

What is *wrong* with you, Pen thought as she took a step back in shock. Where are these thoughts coming from?! Why is there so much venom in you? This isn't you!

Or maybe it *is* you, came the counterthought as Pen glared into the blonde's cool blue eyes. Maybe this was *always* you, and it just took a couple of twists and turns of fate to bring it out in the open. Maybe all that crap about being a peaceful Midwestern farmgirl with kooky ideas about not wanting to slaughter animals for food was all a front, a farce, a fucking mirage.

"I'm sorry," said the blonde, pulling her hand back as if she'd sensed Pen's annoyance. "Where are my manners. I haven't even introduced myself. I'm Charlotte." She straightened up to where she seemed almost a foot taller than Pen, who suddenly felt fat and dumpy in front of this Barbie-doll with perfect hair and teeth. "Charlotte Goodwin," she added, blinking in a way that made Pen realize this woman had rehearsed whatever came next. "*Doctor* Charlotte Goodwin. I'm a professor at the University of North Dakota, and those are my children you just dropped off at school. I'd like them back, please."

## 18

**P**en stared at Doctor Barbie-doll Blondie sitting across the table from her at Rudy's Diner in downtown Fargo. Things seemed weirdly out of place, mismatched, like it just didn't fit. Pen took a breath, feeling a sense of relief when she smelled pancakes, syrup, and fresh coffee in the air. She could tell that this woman hadn't eaten a pancake in at least a decade, and if she ever drank coffee it was probably through a drip or syringe, because there was no other way her teeth could stay that white.

Doctor Charlotte Goodwin, PhD, had suggested they get lunch at an elegant restaurant with tiny tables, big plates, and miniature entrees, but Pen had shaken her head and said no. Rudy's Diner, she'd said.

Her head was spinning and her mind was frazzled. She needed to eat, and she knew Rudy's would fill her up.

Pen waited until the coffee cups were full and the bacon was sizzling in the background, and then she took a breath and looked Doctor Charlotte Goodwin right in the eye. "Let me get this straight," she said, sipping her coffee while holding eye contact. "You're saying you had an agreement with Willow and Randy to adopt their adopted kids."

"Correct," said Charlotte, slowly turning her coffee cup in a circle but making no attempt to raise it to her lips. "I've got all the texts and emails we exchanged about the matter. We hadn't gotten to the point where we'd brought in the lawyers or filed anything official, but we'd come to an agreement. The lawyers were going to be the next step. But then . . ." She paused, placing both hands around the coffee cup and looking into Pen's eyes. "Well, you know." She shook her head. "Unbelievable. Just unbelievable. Such a tragedy."

Pen nodded, looking away for a moment and blinking as she tried to process everything Doctor Charlotte Goodwin had told her on the ride over. At first it didn't make any sense at all: Why in the world would Willow and Randy want to give up the children they'd just adopted?! Willow loved those kids, and she hadn't said a word about giving them up! Not even in passing. Not even when blind drunk.

But Randy . . . well, Randy was different. She'd never been super into being a parent. In their private discussions (which Willow had of course made public to her best friend Pen . . .), it had been agreed that Randy would continue to work full-time while Willow stayed home with the kids. Willow had agreed, with the compromise that she'd take on the occasional catering gig to help with the bills and also to get out of the house once in a while. After all, Willow was a people-person, and she'd always loved catering weddings, graduations, and even funerals. Randy had agreed, but although Willow hadn't really gone into details, Pen had sensed there was some lingering tension about the parental responsibilities. So maybe Randy would consider giving the kids up, especially with Willow gone.

"So you're saying both Willow and Randy were ready to let you adopt the twins?" Pen said slowly, nodding and leaning back on the faux leather as the waitress stormed up with a heaping plate of pancakes, eggs, hash-browns, sausage, and bacon. She smiled as the array of aromas hit her, suddenly making her feel so happy she decided she was in some crazy dream. She dug in, not even bothering to comment on Charlotte's order of one sad-looking gluten-free muffin.

Charlotte shook her head and stared at her muffin. Then she glanced up at Pen. "Just Randy," she said slowly. She carefully unwrapped her muffin and placed it back on the plate. Charlotte hadn't done much with her food but play with it so far, Pen noticed. Weird. But whatever. Weird was about par for the course in her life right now.

"How did you get in touch with Randy? How did the topic come up?"

Charlotte blinked as if surprised at Pen's level of questioning, but she nodded and reached for her bag, pulling out a slim manila folder and placing it on the table. She flipped it open and spun it around so Pen could see it.

"All our emails and texts over the past nine months," she said, clearly pleased with herself for being so organized. Pen hated her already, but the pancakes were too good to hate anything for too long, so she just nodded and shrugged.

"I'll take a look," Pen said, raising an eyebrow when she caught glimpses of texts that sounded pretty darned personal. Stuff Randy had said about Willow, their relationship, their marriage. What the hell?

"Do that," Charlotte said softly, smiling and leaning forward on the table. She reached across and touched Pen's hand, squeezing gently in a way that seemed shockingly intimate in relation to how distant and cold this woman had seemed thus far. What was going on here?

"Uh, yeah," Pen said, drawing her hand back and staring into Charlotte's blue eyes. "That's what I said. Now, are you gonna eat that muffin or shall I put it out of its misery?"

## 19

**I**t is time to put myself out of this misery, said the Sheikh as the wheels of his private jet hit the tarmac at Hector International Airport in Fargo. I have waited three months, but yet this feeling has not left me. And so now it is time to take care of this. To end this misery.

The Sheikh had been ready to saddle up and ride his damned camel to Fargo and his curvy farmgirl, bring her back with him to their Palace the day after she'd left him. He'd been ready to say to hell with those noble intentions, those grand plans, those goals of finishing what his father had been unable to do. So what if the woman had two adopted children? There were a hundred legal tricks and loopholes that could keep them from ever claiming the throne, yes? After all, even if he married Pen, he did not necessarily need to adopt her children! And if there was nothing legal connecting him to the children, then once Zahaar held elections and transitioned its government to democratic rule, even if those kids did grow up and decide they wanted Daddy's throne, there would be little they could do.

Still, Rafeez had held back, telling himself that he would wait three months before making any decisions. He knew better than to make life-changing moves in the heat of anger or the joy of lust, and most certainly the latter was at play with that damned American woman. Ya Allah, he could think of no one else, of nothing else, of no need greater than his need to possess her, to make her his—his woman, his wife, his queen.

The Sheikh hadn't taken a woman to bed in the three months since Pen had walked out of his life and sent two hundred turkeys to Zahaar as a comical reminder of her presence. The desire had been building up in him; but it was a desire for her and her alone. Rafeez couldn't understand it. He'd been infatuated, enamored, and perhaps even been in love before. But not like this. Never like this.

His mind flashed back to Charlotte Goodwin as the plane pulled up to the private gate of the charter terminal. There was no real reason for the thought other than the association it had with her wedding—which was what had brought him to this God-forsaken place in the American Midwest to begin with. He thought of the brief meeting with her new husband, a thin, bespectacled man who barely came up to her shoulders. He seemed pleasant enough, but something had struck the Sheikh as odd about the match. Still, there was no accounting for taste, and besides, what difference did it make why Charlotte had chosen the man she did? It made no difference of course, and so Rafeez pushed it aside and focused on why he was here.

For whom he was here.

## 20

"I am here for you," he said, leaning against the door frame, his large body blocking out most of the light. "I told myself I would wait three months, and now I am here."

Pen blinked up at the dark, muscular figure of the Sheikh. She'd seen his caravan of vehicles drive up to her renovated farmhouse, and after a moment of panic she'd rushed to the bedroom and changed out of her single-mom sweatpants and into some black tights and a top that showed off just enough cleavage that it was sexy without being obscene. Not that she was gonna have sex with him. Nope.

But why not, came the thought as she'd hurriedly dabbed on some makeup and smacked her lips as she checked her look in the mirror. If he shows up at your door with a hard-on and a grin, why is it your responsibility to turn him away again? Why turn him away at all? This isn't the Middle Ages, is it? A man and woman can have sex and then live their own separate lives and have sex again if they feel like it, right? If you hold hands with a man it doesn't mean you're committed to marrying the guy!

"So has something changed or is this just a royal booty call," said Pen, taking a breath as she tried to calm her pounding heart, that pesky heart of hers that whispered—nay, screamed—that this was more than just about her booty.

"Neither," said Rafeez, still grinning. "I am just here to update you on the status of your turkeys."

"How many have you gunned down in cold blood?" said Pen, turning and walking back into the living room, feeling the Sheikh's eyes on her ass as she tried to keep her back arched so her booty would stick out just right. Just in case this *was* a booty call. Which of course it was. She could see it in his eyes. She didn't even need to look at his crotch—though it was hard to miss the bulge.

Pen could feel her own wetness flow into her panties as she caught sight of that old dining table that marked the spot where the Sheikh had tied her like a bound whore, spanked her bottom red and raw, and then stormed out into a snowstorm when she'd asked him to use a condom. What a first date!

She thought back to their second date in the backseat of a golden Range Rover gliding through the Arabian desert, the sand dunes silently watching as she made the king come all over her stomach, once again denying his seed entry into her valley. What a strange courtship, she thought as she felt Rafeez behind her, smelled his distinctive scent fill the room, fill her senses.

Suddenly the thought of him filling her with his seed rushed into her mind, and she turned to him as her arousal burst into full bloom like the sun after a rainstorm. Now she understood why he was here after three months. Sure, this was a booty call. But their entire relationship had been a booty call thus far, hadn't it? His cock. Her booty. What more was there to a relationship? Wasn't she just overthinking it?

Just let him come inside you, she told herself as she looked up at him and smiled. She could feel the fresh lipstick on her face, smell her own perfume in the air. What difference does it make? You're not responsible for this man's choices! So what if you get knocked up and he decides he can't marry you? You're rich. You're already a single mom. And you're ... you're tired. Tired of having to make decisions to uphold someone else's values! Willow's dead. Randy's dead. Willow probably didn't want to give up the twins, but Randy might have. Those emails and texts certainly suggested that Randy was considering Charlotte and her husband's proposal, even if she hadn't agreed yet. And once Willow was gone, wasn't Randy the official guardian, the decision-maker? Wasn't it Pen's moral obligation to uphold Randy's decision to give the twins to Charlotte? For all Pen knew, Willow herself might have agreed if she hadn't been killed. Maybe Willow was already on board but had been too ashamed to admit it to Pen. Who knew?!

"Where are the children?" the Sheikh asked, his voice low as he stepped close to Pen.

"School," said Pen softly. She could feel the arousal flow strong through her. But there was also a sick feeling coursing through her body, a pit in her stomach that she couldn't understand. She wanted to kiss him one moment, throw up the next. What was wrong with her?! Where was all this conflict coming from?!

The Sheikh grunted, leaning in close, his right arm drawing her in, hand sliding down the small of her back and settling on her ass. His crotch was peaked like there was a pipe in his pants, but when he brought his lips to hers she gasped and turned her head, pushing against his chest and stepping back.

"I . . . I can't," she said, closing her eyes and shaking her head furiously, not sure if she was angry with herself or him or Charlotte or Willow or Randy or maybe even those goddamn turkeys with their droopy necks and constant gobbling! "Oh, God, I'm losing my mind," she gasped, her eyes going wide as she gasped again and again, staggering backwards until she was stopped by the old dining table. "Oh, fuck, I'm seriously losing my shit! It's too much. It's just too much! I can't . . . I won't . . . I don't know how to—"

But she couldn't finish the sentence because the Sheikh was on her, his lips smothering hers, his hand sliding around the back of her neck, fingers closing in around her hair, tongue driving into her mouth, hips pushing her legs apart, crotch grinding against her mound.

"It is too much for me too," growled the Sheikh, breaking from the kiss just long enough for her to see in his green eyes that he'd lost control, that whatever had been building over the past three months while they were apart had now been unleashed. She wasn't going to be able to stop him.

And you know what, she thought as she felt both fear and desire whip through her, roiling her insides like the sea in a storm . . . yeah, you know what? Fuck it. I don't wanna stop him.

Pen felt the Sheikh push his hands down her tights from behind, grabbing the waistband of her panties and pulling it up hard, wedging the cloth up inside her rear crack as she gasped and arched her neck back. She was against that sturdy old dining table, and he hoisted her up onto it like she was a doll.

She lay back on the cool wood and spread her legs, groaning as the Sheikh pushed his face into her crotch, licking her through her tights until they were soaked, glistening black satin shining in the yellow light of her living room.

"These need to come off," she muttered, clumsily trying to push her tights down. She was experiencing a profound need to feel the Sheikh's breath against her soft inner thighs, his lips teasing her clit, his tongue curling up inside her vagina. She wanted to feel her juices pour out of her and onto the Sheikh's face, coating him like she was marking him as hers, just like he'd done to her in the backseat of that car three months ago.

"*I* need to come off," the Sheikh whispered, grinning as he raised his head from between her legs and stood up straight, his cock straining to break free from his fitted pants.

"That's a terrible joke, but under the circumstances I'll let it pass without judgment," Pen said with a giggle that quickly turned to a gasp when the Sheikh unbuckled, unzipped, and unleashed.

Suddenly Rafeez was naked in front of her, standing there at the foot of the dining table. His brown, hard, perfectly chiseled body was framed by her spread-out legs, and Pen just stared in awe at the Sheikh's magnificent chest, broad like slabs of marble, his tight brown nipples staring at her like two eyes. The center line of his abdomen was so well-defined she could have counted every muscle along his flat stomach, and the sight of a thick vein curling around his muscular hips made her blink as she finally allowed herself to stare dead-on at his silently throbbing masterpiece of a cock.

Pen's eyes were locked with the massive head of his mast, and although she knew her fingers were still clumsily trying to push those pesky tights down past her hips so she could grant him entry, she couldn't look anywhere but there. At that.

"And what circumstances might those be?" he asked, putting his hands on his hips for a moment before slowly bringing his right hand around and stroking himself until his cock curved upwards, its dark red tip oozing with his clean, natural oil.

"Oh, shit," Pen whimpered as she finally got her tights and panties down past her hips and realized she was soaking wet, dripping all over her dining table like she'd peed herself or something. It was filthy, vulgar, and exciting in a way that made her want to scream out loud, say to hell with the world and all the madness, that this was all she wanted, all she needed. "Please, Rafeez. Please."

The Sheikh stepped closer until his balls were resting on the wooden tabletop, his cock straining as he stroked himself to an erection that seemed primed to explode at any second. Pen glanced up at his face, which was strained with arousal even though his green eyes were open wide and focused on her with a look that sent shivers up and down her body.

"Why are you looking at me like that?" she said, blinking as she realized she was exposed and spread before him, her tights and panties down by her ankles, her top pushed up over her boobs. But she wasn't self-conscious in the least, even though seeing herself in this state of undress generally made her look away from the mirror. The effect this man had on her was incredible. It was uplifting, exciting, arousing . . . and it felt like . . . forever.

And then she understood the look in the Sheikh's eyes. She understood the reason he'd come back. She understood why he'd spontaneously proposed to her three months ago even though it had made no sense. Hell, it still didn't make any sense in a way—not until she looked into his eyes again.

Because his look said forever. You and me, forever.

"I want this," the Sheikh said, exhaling as he glanced down along her curves, his gaze resting on her exposed slit. Pen saw how his breath caught when he looked at her pussy, how his cock flexed, every muscle in his washboard abdomen seizing up as he took in the sight of her sex. "I want this more than I've wanted anything, more than I've wanted anyone. It is more than lust. It is more than the needs of the body. It is the need of a man. The need of a king. I will not deny it any longer under some imagined responsibility, some misguided need to finish what my father could not. This is my need, and I will satisfy it."

Pen's eyelids fluttered as the Sheikh placed both his hands against the insides of her thighs, massaging her sensitive skin, his thumbs resting on the lips of her slit and kneading them open. She moaned wantonly and bucked her hips as she felt herself open up, her wetness pouring out of her, dripping down her slit and forming a dainty little puddle on the table beneath her raised ass.

Her eyes were watering too, and she could only see in flashes as the Sheikh got up on the table, grabbing her thighs firmly and sliding her back so he could get leverage. His cock looked enormous as it bounced between them while the Sheikh got positioned, and then suddenly he was inside her, his entry so silent and smooth Pen almost passed out at the feeling of being stretched and filled without warning.

"Oh, *God*!" she howled, almost choking on the words, her eyes flicking wide open when she realized he was so deep inside her it felt like the first time ever, the *only* time ever! "Oh, Rafeez . . . I can't even . . . oh,*shit*!"

The Sheikh propped himself up on his powerful arms, and then he was pumping into her with all his power, his green eyes locked in on hers, his jawline tight and strained with the effort.

"Ya Allah," he muttered as he rammed into her, pausing for a moment, his neck straining in a way that made Pen think he was coming. But no, he pulled back and began pumping again a moment later, his shaft pushing against the inner walls of her vagina like it was plowing a goddamn tunnel through the center of her body. "It feels like heaven. *You* feel like heaven. I was a fool to deny it, to deny the most natural yearning of a man and woman: To have a child."

Pen looked up at the Sheikh as she felt him flex inside her. She was coming, she realized as she watched this beast of a man above her, images of his muscular body coming through in splinters, like he was a picture put together with stained glass.

Oh, God, I'm coming, she thought again, blinking and then widening her eyes and mouth at the same time. She heard a low wail from somewhere, and it took her a moment to realize it was coming from her, from inside her. She was almost out of her senses as her climax built and built, that low, droning wail rising as the Sheikh drove into her, filling her, stretching her, taking her.

Through her splintered vision she saw Rafeez's eyes roll up in his head, his dark red lips moving as he muttered something under his breath. Again she realized he'd lost himself in her, that his arousal was so extreme he couldn't think of anything but his cock sliding in and out of her, his balls straining to unleash their load. She wanted it, she knew. She could feel her pussy clench and release in time with his powerful strokes. A part of her wanted to wrap her legs around him, press down on his powerful buttocks, milk his cock until he poured everything he had into her depths, filling her until she overflowed onto the goddamn table.

But as her climax continued its slow build to a height that almost scared Pen, she had a moment of strange clarity, a thought that although her body wanted it—and clearly *his* body did too—she needed to stop him. It was her responsibility. It was her duty. It was the reason he'd looked at her like that, like she was his queen, his strength behind the scenes, the woman who could stand beside him, behind him, with him. A woman with the strength to step in and reinforce her king's decisions when he was in danger of losing control.

"No," she whispered, not sure if she was speaking out loud or not. The blood was pounding in her ears as her orgasm incredibly kept going. "Stop, Rafeez. You'll regret it. We both will. It's not worth it. Pull out and finish, Rafeez. Don't compromise on something you've held close for years just to experience a moment of pleasure."

"I am not pulling out," the Sheikh growled, ramming into her so hard she screamed as his hips drove her ass into the hard wood of the tabletop. "This feels right, and I will finish it. Now spread wider for me. There we go. Ya Allah, you are so warm. So bloody tight inside."

Pen was almost out of her mind as she felt herself spread at his command, her thighs pushed outwards as far as they could go. Her face and neck were wet with the Sheikh's kisses, from the way he'd been licking her like an animal as he took her deep and hard. She almost howled in manic laughter as her orgasm reached up and pulled her down with it, pulled her under, made her buck her hips up to meet his entry, clench her pussy when he drove all the way in. She wanted to give in, to give up, to take everything he had. But then again came that thought that there was a reason he'd come back to her, a connection that went beyond that of the body, a duty that came along with being his queen.

So she pushed against his massive chest, trying to stop him from driving back into her. But although Pen was no spindly-armed weakling, even all her strength barely slowed Rafeez down. If anything he went faster, harder, like it was suddenly a race, a competition, a goddamn fight to the finish.

"You have denied me twice," he muttered through gritted teeth. "I will not be denied again. You will take your king deep, and you will take him as often as he wants. Is that clear?"

Pen groaned as she felt him flex inside her, the head

of his curved cock pushing against the front wall of her vagina, dragging its way along as he drove back. She was coming so hard she could barely even see, but somehow the chaos was giving her a single-minded focus that she knew she had to cling to. It was her duty. Her responsibility. It was what would prove she was a queen and not just a whore who bowed her head and quietly obeyed. She'd obey him, but on her terms. She'd obey him like a queen obeys her king.

"Of course I'll take you," she whispered, forcing herself to focus on his eyes. "Look at me, Rafeez. Stop for a moment and look at me. *Look at me!*"

She screamed the last sentence, and perhaps it was the shrillness of her voice, but the Sheikh suddenly stopped in mid-stroke, his green eyes instantly coming into focus.

"Listen to me," she said, holding the eye contact. "Of course I'll take you. As often as you want, as hard as you want, as goddamn deep as you want. And of course I feel the need . . . the same need you feel. But you made a decision for a reason. If you've thought about it and have consciously changed your mind, then that's one thing. But if you're just caught up in the moment, then we might be doing something you'll regret for the rest of your life." She paused and swallowed. "And I can't be the cause of that. I won't be the cause of it."

"You already are both the cause and the effect,"

said the Sheikh. He stroked her hair, his hands slowly moving around to the back of her neck and gripping tight. "You have ignited a need in me that has caused me to question everything. My decisions. My plans. Everything. I want you, Pen. I came here for you. I want you, and—"

"Then *take* me, and me alone," Pen whispered, looking up at him as she suddenly thought of Charlotte Goodwin and that strange conversation about adopting the twins. Those messages between Randy and Charlotte looked real enough, she told herself as she tried to fight the feeling that she was about to do something twisted, horrible, and downright wrong. What kind of a woman gives her kids up for adoption because of a man?! What kind of a woman gives her kids up for*anything*?!

"What do you mean?" said the Sheikh. "You have two children. Do you mean you would be willing to be with me even I do not adopt them as my own?" He blinked and took a breath. "I have considered that option myself. In fact I was ready to suggest it, but now . . ."

"Now what?" Pen said, not sure how to handle that sick feeling rising up in her even as she moved beneath him on the smooth wood tabletop.

Rafeez shook his head. "I cannot do that. If I take you as my queen, I will take everything that comes with you. Everything and everyone. I will not be able to look at myself in the mirror if I turn my back on the children that you have committed to raising on behalf of your friend." He paused, running his hand along her cheek, making her shiver and tremble. "Your friend to whom I will eternally be grateful, Pen. Perhaps it is my duty to help raise her children. Perhaps it is our combined duty. An act of gratitude for bringing us together. It is the right thing to do, and I will do it. Yes?"

Pen stared up at him, not sure what to say. A part of her was warm and glowing inside from what he'd said. But another part of her still felt sick and wretched, and as the Sheikh slowly began to move inside her again, Pen tried to push away the thought that perhaps she herself wasn't doing the right thing. What if Randy and perhaps even Willow really *did* want Charlotte to have those kids? Wouldn't it be wrong for her to ignore that and keep the twins anyway? What was the right thing to do?

What the hell was the right thing to do?!

## 21

"You will marry me. Be my queen. Your adopted children will be our prince and princess. And the children to come will be more princes and princesses," Rafeez said, flexing inside her and driving his powerful hips hard between her thighs. "The transition to democracy will proceed regardless of how many princes and princesses we might have clamoring for the throne of their father. To hell with them. If any of them want to lead the kingdom of Zahaar, they can run for office and earn the right to do so."

The Sheikh pumped harder into her as he spoke, as if his words were powering his drive, his excitement fueled by the new vision forming in his head even as he reveled in the ecstasy of feeling this woman from the inside, deep inside, all the way deep.

A new vision, he thought as he clenched his jaw and felt his balls begin to seize up in preparation for the explosion he could sense coming. An explosion of inspiration. A vision for his kingdom and his personal life all in one. A vision brought into focus by this woman.

His woman.

His queen.

"The vision is true," he whispered as he flexed his buttocks and gripped her head so he could look into her big brown eyes as he came. "I know it. It is perfect. It has all come together because you and I have come together. All the years of denial, the internal conflict, that heavy feeling that I would need to forsake marriage and children for the sake of my kingdom . . . it was misguided. It was an illusion, and your arrival has shattered that illusion. Now I know that the challenge is to raise our children with the same values, the same vision, the same selflessness that I feel, that my father felt but was not able to act on."

He glanced down at her, searching her face for a glimmer of understanding, a sign of agreement, a display of the same joy he was feeling. But instead he saw her pretty round face twisted in turmoil, her eyes clouded by doubt, her lips trembling like she wanted to say something but could not.

"What is it?" he whispered, slowing down even though his balls ached to release their load into her warm valley. "Speak. What is it?"

"It's . . ." she began to say, her eyes filling with tears. "It's . . . oh, God, Rafeez. I'm a horrible person. No matter what choice I make, I'm a horrible person! I can't . . . OK, let me up. I can't let you do this without telling you everything."

She started to talk, and the Sheikh listened, his eyes locked with hers as he lay there on top of her, still connected to her from the inside. Then he heard her mention the name Charlotte Goodwin, and he had to blink and swallow hard.

"Stop," he commanded. "What did you say? What was that name you just mentioned?"

"Charlotte Goodwin. Oh, excuse me: *Doctor* Charlotte Goodwin, PhD. She's a professor or something, not a medical doctor."

"Professor of Middle Eastern Studies," muttered the Sheikh, his head spinning as he slowly peeled himself off Pen and stood upright, naked and hard. His body still wanted Pen, but his mind was elsewhere. Perhaps his mind was nowhere! How in Allah's name did Charlotte get involved in this?

"Actually, I don't know what she teaches," said Pen, as she propped herself up on her elbows and stared at him. "How do *you* know what she teaches?"

"It was Charlotte's wedding that brought me to this

frozen corner of the world to begin with," the Sheikh said, his head still spinning, his mind still running circles around itself as he tried to make sense of what was happening. Was it coincidence? No. Nothing that Charlotte had ever done was coincidence. Everything in her life had been calculated, measured, planned out ... and executed with cold precision. Which made it all the more strange when Rafeez thought about the pieces that didn't seem to fit: The quiet, nondescript man she'd chosen as a husband; this crazy attempt to adopt someone else's adopted kids!

"There is something else going on," muttered the Sheikh. He rubbed his jawline and went to the window. "Because this does not make sense. Charlotte has about as much maternal instinct as a goddamn turkey feather."

"Hey, don't make fun of my turkeys," said Pen from behind him. "They're super protective of their loved ones, and they can get pretty darn fierce when under threat."

The Sheikh turned, smiling and raising an eyebrow when he saw that his curvy queen had slid off the table and was standing before him, naked and perfect. He slid his arm around her waist, pulling her close as the two of them stared out the window. A warmth passed through the Sheikh as he felt how well her curves fit with his body, and even though his mind was still swirling with the revelation of Charlotte's insane attempt to adopt the twins, he felt secure that somehow, someway, he and his queen would figure this out.

Rafeez thought for a bit, and then he sighed and looked down at Pen.

"We need to test the children," he said softly.

"What do you mean? Like a math test? Rafeez, they're children."

"A DNA test. Find out who their real parents are. That must be why Charlotte is so interested in them. Or else why would she want these children and these alone? She does not even know them. We will obtain DNA samples, and then I will have my security people analyze the results."

"Take samples? Excuse me? You're not doing anything of the sort to my children!"

The Sheikh looked into her eyes with all the seriousness he could find. "We will need just a swab of saliva. They are children, Pen. They are probably slobbering all over the place anyway!"

Pen raised an eyebrow and put her hands on her naked hips. "OK, these are my kids we're talking about, not some drooling animals! Can you show some respect, please?"

Rafeez took a breath and raised both hands in defeat. "Ya Allah, I am sorry if I compared your well-mannered children to slobbering beasts. It was not my intention."

"You're the slobbering beast," Pen muttered under her breath, turning away as the Sheikh caught a glimpse of the smile breaking on her pretty round face.

"What was that?" he said, raising an eyebrow and folding his arms over his broad chest.

"Oh, nothing," said Pen, swinging her hips as she walked across the room and reached for her clothes.

"Put those down," the Sheikh ordered.

"Excuse me?"

"Those clothes. Put those down, please. We are not finished here."

Pen blinked as she looked up from the twisted bra she was trying to un-twist so she could cover her boobs. "Um . . . er . . ." she stammered, still holding up the bra as the Sheikh felt his cock rise to full mast so suddenly he felt dizzy again—but this time for a different reason. A purely physical reason.

"Um and er are not words. Who is the inarticulate animal now?" whispered the Sheikh, slowly walking towards her as he saw the arousal express itself in her face, the way her mouth hung open, the way her eyelids fluttered, the way her nipples hardened on their own as he approached.

"I thought . . ." Pen started to say, her words getting swallowed up in a moan as Rafeez walked up to her and simply lowered his head and began to suck her nipples like it was the most natural thing to do under the circumstances. "Oh, God, what are you doing?" she moaned. "I thought . . ."

"There is nothing else to do but wait for your children to finish school, yes?" said the Sheikh, pulling back from her right nipple after slobbering all over it like the beast he was. He pinched her glistening red nib, leaned in and smacked her on the lips, and then proceeded to suck hard on her left nipple under he felt it harden like an arrowhead beneath the circular strokes of his tongue.

"I guess . . ." Pen said, burying her fingers in his hair as he reached around and clawed at her ass while his arousal continued to spiral upwards. "Not that we're gonna do anything even when the kids are done with school. Not before talking about it, at least."

"What is there to talk about?" the Sheikh grunted, lifting his head up from between her breasts. His hands were firmly cupping her rear globes, and he straightened to full height and pushed her back towards that dining table, which was still wet from the way Pen had dripped all over it. "Those children are the key to this. There is something about them that figures into Charlotte's plans, whatever they are."

"Charlotte . . ." Pen muttered, gasping as the Sheikh hoisted her back up on the table. "So you're on a first name basis with Doctor Charlotte Goodwin? Interesting."

"Are you jealous?" said Rafeez, grinning as he

straightened up and glanced down at his cock. "She never got me this hard, you know."

"Ohmygod, so you fucked her!" Pen said, her eyes flicking wide open, her hands grabbing her breasts and covering them up.

"What difference does it make to you?" the Sheikh said, grinning wider as she tried to clamp her thighs together but couldn't because he'd grabbed them and forced her legs apart until she was spread wide in front of him, her scent rising up to his nostrils and driving him wild with need, insane with desire, hot with . . . love? "You refused to marry me anyway. I am just a toy for you. Just a fling. An Arabian ape with the cock of a gorilla. Nothing but a tool for your pleasure and amusement."

"I didn't *refuse* to marry you!" Pen said. "It was a non-starter because I suddenly got two kids out of the blue! I had to walk away, and you had to let me walk away!"

"Well, now I am back," said the Sheikh, slowly climbing on the table, pushing his hips between her legs to force her thighs to stay apart. He grabbed her hands and pulled them away from her breasts, his need escalating to the point where he lost vision for a moment from the sublime sight of her beautiful breasts hanging off to either side, big red nipples pointing outwards in perfect symmetry.

"You're not really back," Pen said, blinking as she

finally stopped struggling and let him hold her down. "Because nothing's changed. I'm not giving up those kids. They're Willow's legacy, and I have to follow through on that. On this."

"They are also my legacy," whispered the Sheikh, leaning in and kissing her lips, slowly moving his face down along her neck.

"What does that mean?"

"I do not know for certain. But it is the only thing that makes sense. Charlotte gets in touch with me after fifteen years of zero contact. At the same time she is secretly trying to adopt the twins."

"How is that the only thing that makes sense? It makes no sense at all. It's pure coincidence."

"Nothing with Charlotte is a coincidence, Pen."

Pen moved her head away from his kiss and pushed against his chest. "OK, stop. What aren't you telling me?"

The Sheikh closed his eyes and took a breath. Then he nodded and looked down at her. "I had an older sister," Rafeez said softly. "She was . . . she was a lost child. I barely knew her. She was found dead from a cocaine overdose. My parents never spoke of her. They pretended like she'd never existed." He paused. "There was a period of time when she left home, was missing, ran away . . . no one knows. I remember because it was a time of great turmoil at the Palace. Then they found her and it seemed like she was on the road to recovery." He shook his head. "A few weeks later they found her in the Eastern Wing of the Royal Palace at sunrise, white powder all over her face, her lips already blue and cold."

Pen stared up at him, her brown eyes wide with shock as she listened. The Sheikh could tell that every ounce of her attention was focused on him, and he felt tears welling up behind his hard, green eyes. Tears that had never flowed before—not for this, at least.

"I'm so, so sorry," she whispered, reaching up and touching his face. She leaned up and kissed his lips, staying silent for another moment before taking a breath. "So you think that maybe she had kids? *These* kids? *My* kids? But that's . . . that's still *way* too far-fetched to make sense, Rafeez! How . . ."

"Those missing years," Rafeez said slowly, blinking as his jaw tightened. "Pen, when my father's investigators finally found my sister, she was in Bogota. Colombia, Pen. How is that for coincidence?"

## 22

Coincidence or conspiracy, thought Pen as she stared up into the Sheikh's green eyes. Suddenly she felt like she didn't know this man anymore, like she'd never known this man.

And I *don't* know him, do I, she thought as fear welled in her throat, making her body seize up as she felt him holding her down with his weight. He showed up on my doorstep in the middle of a goddamn snowstorm. He said Willow sent him to me. But how do I know that for sure? Willow was dead before I ever spoke to her again! Maybe he and Charlotte had been planning this all along! Maybe they'd traced his dead sister's kids, realized they'd been adopted by a couple living in North Dakota, and then tried to re-adopt them from Randy and Willow. Maybe they'd tried legal tricks, bribery, even threats, but Willow said no and so they'd killed her in a fake accident. Then perhaps Randy said no too—after all, who knew if *any* of those emails Charlotte had shown Pen were real—and so they'd killed her in her freakin' bathtub! Didn't that make about as much sense as two people dying in freak accidents within a few months of each other and then a mysterious Sheikh showing up saying his dead sister's kids just *might* be these twins?!

Oh, God, he's gonna kill me and take my kids, Pen thought as she let the fear overtake her, let it push away the last strands of common sense and logic, dismiss the thought that Willow was her best friend and surely she'd have mentioned something if a Middle Eastern Sheikh and a smooth-talking University professor were trying to buy her damned kids from her. Or steal her kids. Or sue her for custody or something.

But it's also possible they never told Willow anything, Pen thought as the Sheikh kissed her gently even as he held her wrists. Maybe they'd profiled Willow as being the stubborn little bitch she was, baby-crazy and in love with her twins. Maybe they'd just quietly gotten her out of the way so they could focus on Randy, and when they couldn't get Randy to give them up, it was on to the next turkey! Penelope Peterson, the farmer who thought she was about to marry a Sheikh!

But if he wanted those kids, why wouldn't he have

just married me when the kids became mine? It would have been so simple, right? Is that what he's trying now? To marry me, get my kids, and then get rid of me? Or maybe . . .

No, Pen thought firmly as she blinked and searched Rafeez's handsome brown face for some sign to reassure her that he wasn't a psycho. No, she thought again.

"You want to kill them, don't you?" she whispered softly, the dread making it hard for her to speak.

"What?" said the Sheikh, cocking his head and frowning. "What did you just ask me?"

"Your sister's kids. You want them dead. It's part of this crazy determination not to leave behind any descendants so no one will ever be able to claim Zahaar's throne after you start to transition the kingdom to democracy. All this . . . *all* of this is just some twisted, fucked-up, insane plan to adopt your sister's kids and then quietly get rid of them!"

Rafeez stared down at her for several long moments, his green eyes wide as if he was trying to process what the hell she was talking about. Then he blinked as if he'd pieced together her theory, finally smiling in a way that seemed far too cool for Pen's comfort.

"Let me make sure I am understanding this correctly," he said slowly, still holding her wrists down, his smile widening to a grin that almost angered Pen because it smacked of condescension, perhaps even pity—like he thought she'd lost her mind or perhaps was some crazy chick who's just gotten her period. To hell with this ape, she thought obstinately as she was forced to listen.

"Go ahead," she said. "Make sure you are understanding this correctly. You speak English, don't you? You went to Oxford University, didn't you? With Charlotte Goodwin? You played doctor with her back then, didn't ya? And now you want to play God! With *my* kids! Fuck you, you madman! Let me up!"

The Sheikh snorted with incredulous laughter, and for a moment Pen had to admit he looked genuinely shocked, perhaps even shaken. But then that lazy confidence of a king in control was back, and he just shook his head and stayed on her, pinning her down with his weight and strength.

"So you believe that I killed your friend and her spouse in some convoluted plan to get to my dead sister's children so I could kill them too? If I could engineer two separate fake accidents, why would I not simply have the twins killed in an accident too? Why not just one nice big fake car accident that took care of all of them?"

Pen blinked up at the Sheikh. What he said did make sense, but that didn't mean she was wrong. "Insane, power-mad villains don't always use logic," she said. "Have you ever watched a James Bond movie where the bad guy invents some elaborate machine to kill Bond instead of just putting a bullet in his head and ending it?"

The Sheikh snorted again, leaning in so close she could almost taste him. Or perhaps she could still taste him from the way he'd kissed her earlier. Or was that herself she was tasting from where his lips had been?

"So this is a spy thriller, is it?" he said softly, tightening his grip on her wrists and moving even closer to her mouth. "I thought it was a romance story."

"Romance stories have happy endings," Pen said, shaking her head as she felt the arousal start to wind its way up along her naked thighs. The Sheikh was hardening against her soft, wet mound, his cock lining up along her slit as it filled out. "And there's no way this story ends well."

The Sheikh grunted, kissing her neck and making her shudder. "Well, perhaps we are not at the end yet, my curvy heroine."

Pen closed her eyes and arched her back, the little voice that whispered she was crazy getting softer as her arousal grew stronger. "Well, we'd better get a move on towards the climax, don't you think?"

Rafeez laughed as he kissed her full on the lips, and as Pen kissed him back she decided that she was as crazy as he was, that she was kissing a man who very well might have had two people murdered, a man who could easily have her killed without a trace—a man who was strong enough to kill her himself without breaking a sweat!

Suddenly the Sheikh pulled back from the kiss and flipped Pen over on the table. The breath was squeezed out of her lungs as she felt his weight press down on her back, squishing her boobs up into her chest. Then he was kissing her neck and shoulders furiously, rubbing her arms and back, running his hands all over her body from behind as he ripped off the last strands of her clothing until she was buck naked, spread face-down before him.

"Yes," he muttered from behind her, and Pen gasped when she heard how his words were almost unintelligible because his voice was so thick with arousal. "The climax. Now it occurs to me that I have not yet come inside you. I am no expert, but don't most romance novels begin with the hero putting his heroic seed into the hapless woman, after which drama ensues until they accept their destiny?"

"Well," groaned Pen as she arched her back and raised her ass, reveling in the way the Sheikh was massaging her curves from behind, "there's all kinds of romance plots."

"So which one is this? The Sheikh Romance?" whispered the Sheikh as he kissed the small of her back, sending tingles down her heavy thighs as she felt his warm lips move close to the ridge above her rear crack. "The one that fetishizes virile Arabian men and their savage ways? The one where the heroine thinks she has fallen in love with a beast who cares not for anything other than his pleasure." He paused, slowly spreading her rear cheeks and making Pen wet as she realized he was staring directly at her rear pucker. "His pleasure . . ." whispered the Sheikh, his breath feeling warm against her most private, untouched space. "Which he takes when he wants, how he wants . . . and *where* he wants."

And before she realized what was happening Rafeez had pushed his face down between her rear globes, and when she felt his tongue circle her dark hole and then slide inside in the most filthy, dominant way, Pen knew what was coming. She also knew she couldn't stop it if she tried.

The Sheikh licked her for several long, silent moments. Then he drew his tongue back out of her rear and grabbed her hips, forcing her to raise her ass. He smacked her hard on each buttcheek until she felt the sting ripple through her, and Pen knew that she wasn't gonna try to stop him. She was going to take his climax wherever he wanted to give it to her.

## 23

"You know this is only reinforcing the stereotypes about Arabian heroes in Sheikh Romances," she said, turning her head halfway and glancing back at Rafeez as he pulled back from licking her rear and stared at her glistening dark ring.

"If I am a stereotype, then so are you, my dear," the Sheikh replied, his jaw tightening as he looked at her pretty face half-turned towards him, her brown eyes misty with arousal. He loved her, he decided in that moment. It was a simple thought, clear and precise. He loved her, and she loved him. There was no other explanation. After all, she'd just accused him of murder, conspiracy, a plot to kidnap children, and of being a goddamn James Bond supervillain. And yet she was spread before him, arching her back and raising her rump while he licked her clean, tight little asshole until it shone like a beacon.

"Oh, really?" she said, gasping as he smacked her ass again. "What stereotype is that?"

"The conservative, innocent Western woman who does not understand why this animal from Arabia is awakening such lust in her curvy body," he replied, smacking her ass once more and feeling his cock getting even harder as he watched her magnificent rear globes shudder and turn bright red from the spanking. "The mild mannered housewife who loses control in the heat of passion and finds herself spread naked and wide on her own dining table while her children are at school. The virginal farmgirl who has no idea what to do with all the wet holes in her blossoming body."

Pen snorted with laughter, half-turning again as the Sheikh rubbed her ass, pulling her globes apart and then letting go so they shuddered as her crack closed up again. "First of all, that's like three different stereotypes. Secondly, there you go using the word virginal in a sentence. And thirdly . . . thirdly . . . oh, God, Rafeez, what are you doing?"

The Sheikh had driven his long, thick middle finger into her asshole as Pen spoke, and now he curled two fingers of his other hand up inside her cunt from below. "Showing you what these wet holes of yours are for, my lady," he whispered as he slowly began to move all fingers at once.

She came almost instantly, her body seizing up as her wetness poured down his hand. The groan she emitted was so primal, so surreal, so beautiful that the Sheikh almost exploded without his cock being touched. It felt so good, so right, so bloody perfect that he almost shouted out loud in joy.

"I love you," he whispered, still plumbing both her holes with his fingers, gently and with care so he wouldn't hurt her. She was coming so hard Rafeez wasn't sure if she'd heard him, and so he leaned in closer, driving that middle finger deeper into her anus as he said it again: "I love you, Pen. I know nothing makes sense right now, but we will make sense of it together. Together."

She gasped as the Sheikh's finger went all the way inside, down to the knuckle. He held it there as he fucked her pussy with his other hand, breathing deep of her scent as she came again for him.

"Do you love me?" he whispered in her ear from behind, moving up on his knees and leaning over as he felt the need in his balls rivaled only by this sudden need in his heart. The need to hear her say she loved him. It seemed trivial, almost a joke. But the Sheikh also realized that the only thing that would get them through whatever was happening here was trust. Trust, which was just another word for love.

"Do you trust me?" he whispered, slowly pulling

his finger out of her rear and looking around the open kitchen of the newly renovated farmhouse. There were kids' toys everywhere, and the Sheikh felt strange when he considered the possibility that the children who lived here shared his blood. He had no way of knowing that without running tests, of course. But it seemed right. Why else would Charlotte want these children and these alone?

Then Rafeez felt a catch in his throat, and he blinked and shook his head. He was going insane. It was all just a coincidence, he told himself. His sister had never had children, because if she had, Rafeez would already know about them. Certainly his father had his security and intelligence personnel investigate at the time. Rafeez himself had ordered in-depth research of the Al-Zahaar bloodline to make sure there were no offshoots close enough to ever contest the throne if Rafeez did not father any children. If his own intelligence people had come up blank, how in Allah's name could Charlotte Goodwin have discovered that his sister had given birth to twins? And who was the father?

Rafeez's mind went back to that thin, bespectacled man who'd stood beside Charlotte at the wedding as if he were just part of the background instead of the groom. But of course he could not be the twins' father—if he were, there would be no need for Charlotte to do all that wheeling and dealing to get those children. She could have just showed that her husband was their birth father, and that would have been solid moral ground—if not legal—to ask for custody of the twins.

So is it just coincidence, the Sheikh thought again as he bent over and kissed Pen's twin rear cheeks, the left and then the right, tracing his finger along her crack one last time before he climbed off the table and walked to the small shelf near the large stove in the open kitchen. He scanned the items on there, smiling and nodding when he saw that Pen was well-stocked with organic coconut oil. He grabbed the jar and headed back to the table, where Pen was lying face down now, exhausted and still panting as she looked at him sideways.

"What's that for?" she said, raising an eyebrow. "Um, *what* is that for?!"

"I am asking the questions here," said Rafeez, grinning as he patted her buttocks and then smacked her once with his open palm.

"Ouch," she giggled. "All right. What's the question."

"First I asked if you love me," said the Sheikh as he unscrewed the top of the jar and placed it on the table. He smacked her ass again, holding his palm against her skin and rubbing until her breathing told him she was getting aroused again after her climax. "And you said nothing."

"Because you were doing those things to me with

your fingers," she whispered. "I could barely see, let alone speak!"

"You can see now, yes? You can speak now, yes?"

Slowly Pen nodded as the Sheikh massaged her big bottom, his cock so peaked that he was afraid he would explode like a goddamn fountain, blasting his load all over her naked rump like he was a geyser in season. No. This time he was finishing inside her. His way.

"Yeah, I can speak . . . kinda, I guess," she whimpered as the Sheikh pulled her rear globes apart and glanced at her hole, tight and clean, puckered and perfect. Just for him. For him alone.

The madness of what was happening almost made the Sheikh stagger on his feet as he coated his fingers with the coconut oil and then began to circle her rim with the natural lubricant. The invitation to Charlotte's wedding, two accidental deaths, the curious case of the twins . . . there had to be a connection. It could not all be coincidence, could it?

Rafeez looked down at Pen's pretty round face as he circled her rim with his thumb and forefingers. Her eyes were closed, her mouth twisted in a grimace of pure ecstasy. A few minutes ago she'd accused him of plotting all of it along with Charlotte—some twisted plan to take her kids from her and then kill them or something—or perhaps kill her! And now she was arching her back and spreading her ass for his fingers, soon his cock.

Ya Allah, Rafeez thought as he stared in wonder at her closed eyes. Perhaps I am the one who is being played here! Perhaps there is indeed a conspiracy, and it is all being masterminded by this American farmgirl! Perhaps I am the target here! After all, if the twins are indeed my sister's blood, part of the Royal Al-Zahaar bloodline, then if I am killed, they will have an uncontested path to the throne! Perhaps this woman writhing and moaning at my touch is behind all of it! Perhaps it is she who discovered the identity of the children's birth parents, had both Willow and Randy killed, and then made up some story about Charlotte to confuse me!

Perhaps Charlotte was never involved at all, the Sheikh wondered as he pushed one finger into Pen's asshole.

Perhaps Willow and Randy have not even been killed, the Sheikh thought as his eyes widened in tandem with the way Pen's rear hole widened when he pushed a second finger into her.

Perhaps the twins did not even exist, the Sheikh decided as his vision clouded over and he began to drive his fingers into her rear with a fury that made Pen's ass tighten around his fingers. Perhaps it was just a plan for her to get pregnant with his child and then have him eliminated! Maybe *all* these women had manufactured this twisted plan to steal his kingdom!

Yes, he thought: Perhaps this farmgirl is not what she seems. All that nonsense about having me pull out was just an act, a tease, a show, a build-up to the final phase! Perhaps she was not in the most fertile stage of her cycle when I arrived at her doorstep that time, and she wants to make sure I come inside her when the chances of her taking my seed are highest!

The paranoia was rising along with his cock, and the Sheikh was now certain he was going insane. Perhaps that was his father's true gift to the son: Madness, pure and simple! Who knew?!

"Tell me the truth," he growled as he slid a third finger into her rear and pumped deep and hard, making her moan as her anus tightened and then was forced to open up for him. "Whose idea was this?"

"What?" she gasped. "What idea?"

"Shut up and answer me," he growled, stroking his cock with the other hand as he watched his fingers disappear knuckle-deep between her asscheeks.

"How can I shut up and answer at the same time?" she whispered. "That's physically impossible, genius."

The Sheikh would have laughed if he hadn't been so far gone in his paranoia, if his arousal hadn't become so all-encompassing, if the back-and-forth between coincidence and conspiracy wasn't so damned confusing.

"I will show you what is physically impossible," he grunted, pulling his fingers out and forcing her to raise her ass by smacking her hard on the rump. In a moment he was up on the table, on his knees behind her, forcing the massive head of his cock into her asshole before it could close up again.

"Oh, *God*!" she screamed as the Sheikh watched his thick brown shaft disappear all the way into her, sliding easily between her large rear globes until he was balls deep inside his farmgirl. "Oh . . . oh . . . I . . . I can't."

"You can and you will," the Sheikh said as he began to pump, arching his neck back as he let the arousal take over. "And by God, you already have."

## 24

**T**he arousal took over once Pen got past the initial shock of his sudden, forceful entry. She'd been on the verge of orgasm even when the Sheikh pushed that third finger into her, and it came as she felt herself stretched so wide she was sure a train could drive through there.

"Oh, my God," she groaned as her climax hit as the Sheikh dug his fingers into her rear cushion and drove in so hard she felt the vibrations through every ounce of convulsing flesh. Again the thought came that this was some kind of twisted conspiracy, but then the thought was gone as her orgasm reached up from the darkness and pulled her down again.

Pen almost choked as the Sheikh flexed inside her, the upward curve of his massive cock touching her in places so deep, so dark, so untouched that she didn't know if she was coming or dying.

She felt his balls against her ass as he fucked her, heard him mutter in Arabic, the strange words coming through between his groans and grunts. For a moment she felt she was being taken by some mythical beast, the fleshy avatar of the God-king himself, and when she heard him roar as he prepared to deliver his load into her, Pen was suddenly certain he was going to impregnate her from the rear, the two of them creating some unnatural hybrid of god, man, and beast that would rule the world with an iron claw!

The image was so ridiculous that Pen almost laughed out loud. But she was so far gone that it seemed to make as much sense as anything else in her world, and so she just arched her back down, spread her thighs farther apart, and reached back between her legs for the Sheikh's balls.

She found them, and immediately he slowed down and roared again in primal pleasure as she cupped them and moved back and forth.

"Ya Allah, you witch," he groaned. "Ibd din allahi. What are you doing to me?! Who are you?!"

"I don't know," she muttered, realizing that she was speaking the truth. "I don't know who I am."

I really don't, she thought as she massaged Rafeez's balls while he rhythmically drove into her anus, the coconut oil dripping out of her crack and down his thick shaft, coating her hands in a wonderfully filthy way.

And then he came inside her, hard and with power, deep inside her just as she wondered how it was she'd ended up here, godmother to two kids, whore to a Middle-Eastern Sheikh . . .

"Oh, God," she howled as she felt his heat explode so far inside her she thought she could taste it. She pulled on his balls furiously as he flexed inside her, his cock pushing against the inner walls of her rear canal, stretching them wider than she thought was natural.

But she was taking it, her body was taking it, taking him, all of him.

"Ya Allah," he shouted, pulling back and then ramming himself in, pouring a fresh load of his semen into her as he dug his fingers into her sides, his hips pressed tight against her ass. "It feels so bloody good. It has never felt like this. Never."

"Never," she repeated, her body somehow numb but fully alive with tingles all at once, every ounce of her filled with his energy just like her rear was filled with his seed. "Never."

The Sheikh pumped until he was emptied, and then slowly he pulled out. Pen exhaled once and then sighed as she wondered if she'd ever close up again, she'd been stretched so wide by his girth, plumbed so deep with his length. He pushed her face down on the table, collapsing on top of her, his body feeling like a blanket. He kissed her hair, nuzzled against the back of her neck, whispered in Arabic in her ear.

"Ibd din allahi," he said.

"What does that mean?" she asked, her words slurring when she realized that in all the chaos she herself had come again, even though she wasn't sure how that was possible while being taken from behind.

"Ibd din allahi? It simply means I love you."

Pen giggled. "You know, I read once that the only time a man is completely honest is the three minutes after he's blown his load. Apparently that's the only time he isn't thinking about sex and how to get it."

The Sheikh grunted. "Well, I am already thinking about sex. About which hole to take you in next. Part of your education, you see."

Pen felt herself blush as she became conscious that his semen was still warm inside her. It would ooze out when she turned over. It would probably drip out of her all day. What would those parents and teachers think when she showed up at school to pick up her kids? Would they know that this single-mom's panties were damp from a Middle-Eastern Sheikh's royal seed?

"Shit, I need to pick up the kids soon," Pen groaned, turning to look at the time. "Yup. I should get cleaned up. Get off me, you big oaf. God, you're heavy!"

The Sheikh made no move to get off her. "You still have some time, yes? How far away is the school?"

"Not far. About ten miles down Highway 95."

"Public school?"

"No. This is a private school that's highly rated."

"Sounds expensive," said the Sheikh. "At least your turkeys are not dying in vain."

Pen tried to turn so she could see if he was joking or not. She couldn't tell from his deadpan voice. "Tell me you're joking. You haven't seriously been hunting my turkeys, have you?"

The Sheikh leaned close and kissed her hair. "I am giving them some time to get used to their new habitat. Get the lay of the land. Exercise their muscles, which have become soft and flaccid from a life of ease and luxury in America."

"*You're* soft and flaccid," she teased, struggling once again to turn. But the Sheikh felt like he was getting heavier, and she finally sighed and gave up. "All right. At some point you need to let me up. Wait, what are you doing? Rafeez? *Rafeez!*"

Pen screamed as the Sheikh grabbed her wrists and rolled off her, pulling her up as he landed on his feet. He yanked her against his body, holding her arms down in a bear hug and wrestling her over to the radiator pipes that lined the wall of the old farmhouse.

"Ibd din allahi!" he shouted. "Ibd din allahi!"

Suddenly the front door burst open and two veiled

*Grateful for the Sheikh*

women rushed in. Pen stared in disbelief as the Sheikh barked out orders to them in Arabic while he held her tight against the wall. One of the women nodded and walked briskly out the door. The other stood silently and stared unblinkingly as Pen felt suddenly self-conscious at being buck naked like a goddamn white cow.

"Are you fucking insane?" she gasped when the first woman returned carrying what looked like smooth nylon rope. "What the hell do you think you're doing?"

"These women will stay with you to make sure you do not injure yourself," the Sheikh said calmly, nodding at the women as he held her wrists out so they could tie her to the radiator pipes. "Once I am out of the country, they will untie you."

"Oh, God, you're insane," Pen muttered, her eyes going wide as she tugged at the knots and realized they were secure. She was tied good and tight. "Oh, God, I should have my head examined for letting you in. I knew you were insane the moment you walked into my life, and—"

"Call me what you want," Rafeez said calmly as he dressed and then pointed at a thin throw-blanket draped over a chair. One of the attendants grabbed the blanket and covered Pen's nakedness with it. The Sheikh continued as he nonchalantly tied his shoes. "But I was honest with you in that moment. I do love you. I just cannot be sure if I trust you. Not yet. Not until I solve the puzzle of these children. And I cannot do that here. I need to take them back to Zahaar."

Pen almost choked when she realized what he was doing, what he was planning to do. He'd asked her about the school. So now he knew it was a private school about ten miles down the highway. That would pretty much narrow it down—assuming he didn't already know which school they attended!

"You can't just go and pick up my children," she said, her eyes wide as she stared at the Sheikh. "They won't release my kids to just anyone! You need to have an ID card authorizing you. There's no way this will work, you dumb ape! Now untie me and maybe . . . just *maybe* I won't have you arrested!"

Rafeez grinned and shook his head. "What do you have against apes? Tsk. Tsk. So judgmental."

"Ohmygod, you're a psycho," Pen groaned, pulling on the nylon rope until she felt the pipes creak. But she'd had them bracketed tight to the wall when the house was renovated, and they wouldn't break. Not before her damned wrists broke, anyway. "All right, look. This isn't gonna work. No way the school releases my kids to a stranger. And if you drive up in a caravan of shiny black cars and demand they be released to you, the school is going to call me. When I don't answer, they'll call the police, who will head right over here and bust through this door."

The Sheikh finished tying his bespoke leather shoes. Then he carefully straightened the cuffs and creases of his tailored trousers before standing up and raising an eyebrow. "So it appears we have a problem. What do you propose?"

Pen glanced at her bound wrists and back at him. "I propose you untie me, walk out that door, and disappear back to your sandpit and sandcastles."

"Not acceptable. Try again."

"What do you mean, try again? This isn't a game show! These are my kids we're talking about!"

"And they may also be *my* kids!" Rafeez said, his jaw going tight. "If they are my sister's blood, then they become my responsibility. I have to know." He paused, folding his arms across his broad chest and taking a step towards her. "*You* have to know too. Because Charlotte already knows something we don't, and trust me, that woman plans everything out to the last detail. So try again. Since I am a dumb ape and you are the brains of this operation, go ahead and try again. What do you propose?"

Pen closed her eyes and exhaled slowly, her heart racing as she realized where the Sheikh was leading her, what he wanted her to say. And she knew she had to say it. She had to agree. He was right. If these were indeed his dead sister's kids, he had the right to know. And hell, if this bitch Charlotte started some kind of legal trouble using those emails and texts from Randy as proof that there was an adoption agreement, it would help to have the Sheikh in her corner, wouldn't it?

Again Pen wondered if she was being played, if this

was all being engineered by the Sheikh and Charlotte. Perhaps he'd already arranged for fake DNA results. Or perhaps he'd decided to kill the kids if they did turn out to be his sister's. Or maybe Rafeez and Charlotte would just kill*her* and live happily ever after in a sandcastle with Willow's children!

I want to live in a sandcastle, Pen suddenly thought as her mind swirled and her body tensed up with a strange longing. Away from this madness and depravity. Away from . . . him.

But she couldn't sustain the thought, because at the heart of it she knew the last part wasn't true. She didn't want to be away from him, psycho or not, big dumb ape or not. Although she shouldn't trust him, she did. And although she couldn't possibly love him, she did.

Oh, God, I love him, she thought as she looked at her bound wrists, felt his seed drip out of her. It sounded mad, depraved, sick. But it was true. She trusted him from the moment she'd let him walk through her door in that snowstorm. Willow had sent him to her, and now she was wealthy, with two wonderful kids, and in love with a Sheikh! Sure, she was tied up and her ass was still stinging from being spanked so hard, but there was a feeling of warmth flowing through her as she put things in perspective.

We both had our moments of doubt. We both still can't be sure if the other one is being honest. But we can't deny that there's something in the air when the two of us are together. A spark. An electricity. A sense of connection that just can't be denied.

"All right," she said, feeling that electricity flow through her when she understood that the Sheikh wasn't stupid enough to actually drive up to an American school and expect to bundle up two kids and shove them into his limousine without being taken down with extreme prejudice. He wanted her to say it. He wanted her to make the choice. The choice to trust him. "All right. I'll do it. I'll go with you. We'll pick up the kids together." She took a breath and nodded. "And we'll run the DNA tests. Settle this matter once and for all."

## 25

"I still don't understand why we had to fly to Zahaar to settle this," Pen said softly as she watched the twins gently snore, their mouths wide open as they lay tucked cozily in blankets in the large leather recliners of the Sheikh's private jet. "We do have DNA testing facilities in America, you know."

"It is not the DNA tests per se," said Rafeez. He'd been watching the twins sleep for at least an hour. Just watching calmly, his green eyes unwavering, completely focused on them. Pen had wondered what he was thinking, but she'd stayed quiet and let him be alone with his thoughts. In a way she'd known what he was thinking. She'd been thinking the same thing: What happens if they confirm that the children are related to him? If they are indeed his sister's children? What happens then?

"What do you mean?" Pen said, her eyes still focused on how the Sheikh was staring at the children. For a moment she thought of the animal kingdom, where many male animals will kill the young fathered by another male just to make sure their own seed prevails. But then she blinked away the thought and shook her head.

"I mean once we get the DNA results from the children's saliva swabs, we will need to compare them with the DNA records of the royal Zahaari bloodline. I checked with my people back in Zahaar, and we have no DNA sample from my sister. We have very few medical records of her. My parents were ashamed of her addictions, her weakness. It is sad, but that is the situation. If we had records, it would be a simple comparison: The DNA records would show a fifty-percent match between the child and the mother, and that would be the end of the matter. But now we will need to test the DNA results against my own sample. And it gets complicated because my sister and I do not share the same mother. I want to make sure I am there to supervise the analysis, to be involved every step of the way." He took a breath. "And if necessary, to order an exhumation."

"Wait, what?"

The Sheikh shrugged as he silently gestured to an attendant, who disappeared and then almost immediately returned with a tray of steaming hot sweet tea. "Muslims bury our dead just like Christians do, Pen. My sister died of an overdose in the Royal Palace. She is buried in the Royal graveyard on the Palace grounds, along with the rest of my family. It is considered heresy to dig up the grave of a dead royal, but I will have it done if needed."

Pen closed her eyes and exhaled. "I still think we could have settled this without pulling my kids out of school and flying halfway across the world. But all right. We're here now, I suppose."

She went quiet as she watched the Sheikh sip his tea. The twins had taken to him instantly, both of them delighted to ride in a limousine that had a fridge and a candy-closet and enough space to run around even though Pen had ordered them to stay seated and strapped in while the car was moving. Getting on the private jet had the kids squealing in delight, and it was only then that Pen realized that other than the very first trip to the United States from Colombia, these children had never even seen an airplane up close.

"It is very important to keep your seatbelt on while we are flying," the Sheikh had told each of the twins. "If you want anything, just snap your fingers and one of my attendants will bring it for you."

"Mike and Ike's?"

"Gummi squids?"

"I do not know what those are," the Sheikh had said, scratching his head and making the kids laugh. "But my attendants will get them for you or else I will have them thrown off the plane."

"Hey now," Pen had said hurriedly. "Let's not give them the wrong idea about how the world works. No snapping fingers to summon attendants. Show respect to people and they will respect you back. As for throwing people out of airplanes for not being stocked with gummi squids . . . hmmm . . . all right, I guess I see the logic there."

They'd all laughed as the twins snapped their fingers like it was a Spanish dance party. The attendants joined in the fun, and somehow produced both Mike and Ike's and gummi squids for the kids, much to the Sheikh's surprise.

"I will have to closely inspect the list of items we carry on board," he told his head attendant sternly. "There is no logical reason for us to have these . . . these *things* in stock in the galley! Ya Allah, that is an octopus made out of sugar! As for this thing called Mike and Ike . . . by God, it makes my mouth pucker up like a fish dying a horrible death!"

"OK, can we stop talking about throwing people from airplanes and fish suffocating to death, please?" Pen said to the Sheikh even though she was beaming as she said it. It had occurred to her then that this entire trip wasn't so much about the DNA results as it was about something else. It was about them. All of them.

And now as she watched the Sheikh sip his tea, the steam from the pot swirling through the air like white fingers before dissipating, Pen decided that yes, this was about them. Sure, the DNA results were important, but certainly all of that could have been done without flying to Zahaar. This itself was the test, wasn't it!

A test in the form of a family vacation!

He wants this experience, doesn't he, she thought as she continued to watch the Sheikh watching the kids like they were his own. The experience of fatherhood, of raising children, of being a role model to individuals alongside his broader responsibility of being a role model to his kingdom. This is just an excuse for him to see what it's like to be the head of a family, not just a country.

But does he just want a taste, or will he want it forever, Pen wondered as she felt the butterflies in her stomach as the plane slowly began its descent towards Zahaar. What happens if they're his sister's kids? What happens if they aren't? Does it even matter? He's already made a vow—in private and in public—that he'll never be a father, never have an heir. So what's the endgame here? What's his plan? Was I wrong to trust him? Was I wrong to trust Willow's opinion of him? Was I wrong to trust my body? Is the only reason he's flying us all to Zahaar that he can get rid of us in a place where he has absolute control? Are there going to be three unmarked graves somewhere in the Royal Graveyard at the end of this "family" vacation?

Her thoughts rolled back to Charlotte Goodwin again, then the strange "accidental" deaths of Willow and Randy. Whatever was happening here was clearly important enough for death to be an option. Sure, there'd been no indication of foul play; but the coincidence was too much. Just too much to be believed. But who the hell was capable of engineering two accidental deaths that fooled the police detectives? The cops weren't morons. They would have been troubled by the coincidence as well. Clearly they didn't find any evidence in either the car accident or the bathtub drowning.

The butterflies were going nuts as the plane swooped in for a smooth landing, but alongside the fear was still that warm glow as Pen watched the Sheikh lean over and comfort the kids, who'd both woken up as the plane's wheels hit the tarmac. She thought of her turkeys and what the Sheikh had said when he made that ridiculous proposal: What kind of life is it for those birds to wake up with nothing to look forward to but their daily feeding? Is it not better for them to live free and wild, even with the threat of being hunted by a predator?

Is that why I'm still playing this game with a man

who could turn on me, turn on all of us, Pen wondered. Because I'd rather be the turkey that takes the risk, chooses to live free and wild instead of in a prison that's safe and secure but routine and dull? Is that why I'm still here? Is that why I feel this warm glow alongside the fear? Is that why I feel grateful alongside being scared for my children, for myself, for what's to come?

Be grateful, she told herself, narrowing her eyes and smiling as she basked in the image of the Sheikh carefully unbuckling the kids and helping them unravel their blankets, find their shoes, and get ready for whatever came next.

## 26

"What comes next?" the Sheikh said, setting his jaw as he stared at the papers handed to him by the Royal Medical Examiner. "What other tests should we run to be sure?"

The Medical Examiner blinked, bowing his head almost instinctively. "There are no other tests, Sheikh. The results are clear and indisputable. We have run them three times, even taking new samples just to make sure nothing was contaminated in the process. I personally supervised every step of the process. There is no doubt these results are accurate." He swallowed hard and made brief eye contact with the Sheikh before lowering his gaze to the intricately designed Persian rug. "The match between you and the children is zero percent. You share no blood with the children. They are not part of the Royal Zahaari Bloodline, Sheikh. They cannot be your sister's children."

The Sheikh tossed the papers down on the low teakwood table on which he'd been resting his bare feet. He frowned as he tried to interpret the strange feelings flowing through him as he heard the news. This was good news, wasn't it? Was it? Ya Allah, suddenly he did not know! He did not know what he wanted! He did not know anything at all!

Rafeez waved away the Medical Examiner and rubbed his stubble as he looked over at Pen and the twins standing on the open balcony at the far end of the sprawling day chambers that were reserved for the Sheikh's Royal Family. They look like they belong here, he thought. Like they belong in this palace. Belong in this world. Belong with me.

I was certain they were my blood, he thought as he finally acknowledged that at the bottom of it he was disappointed, shattered, broken by the news that they were not bound to him by blood. He'd almost welcomed the idea of being trapped by the situation, forced to take responsibility for the children, relieved of the burden of deciding for himself. If they were his dead sister's children, there was no choice to make, yes? He had to step up and take on the responsibility. Take on the responsibility for all of them.

*I want this,* the Sheikh thought as he watched Pen laugh at something one of the twins said and then point at one of the minarets that reached up to the sky from the bustling city beyond the palace walls. *Ya Allah, I want this.*

Pen turned just in time to catch him looking at her, and the Sheikh felt himself smile as he gazed into her brown eyes. How in Allah's name had she stuck it out with him thus far? Obviously she had her doubts about him, his intentions, perhaps even his sanity. But here she was, standing there in a long, flowing white dress with a black head scarf, looking like his queen already. His queen, standing there and looking at him, his prince and princess by her side.

"I want this," the Sheikh muttered. "I want it all. I will hold good to my promise to the kingdom, but I will not sacrifice the basic needs of a man to do it. That is all. That is my decision. We will find a way to have it all. Me and my queen."

But the moment Rafeez whispered those words to himself, a sudden dread caught hold of him and he blinked and frowned as he wondered what it was.

Fear, he realized as he studied himself and then glanced back at Pen. *Fear that once I tell her the children are not my blood, she will pack up and leave. After all, why would she stay? She has a comfortable life in America. Her financial future is secure. Yes, we have a connection. Yes, there is chemistry between us. But* she also knows that I have power and influence, and that if these children were born of my dead sister, I would stop at nothing to get them. Perhaps that is the only reason she is here: To protect her children. Perhaps she reasoned that instead of me kidnapping them, it is better that she willingly plays along . . . plays along until she no longer has to play along.

"What is it?" came her voice, breaking Rafeez from his daydream. He looked up to see his wide-hipped American farmgirl walking towards him, the twins holding on to her skirts on either side. She looks like a picture of divine motherhood, thought the Sheikh as he watched the warm desert breeze blow her scarf back and play with her long brown hair as she giggled and tried to set it right.

The Sheikh looked directly into her eyes and smiled. Then he glanced at the twins, a chill rising up in him when he realized what he was going to do. Finally he looked back up at Pen's pretty round face.

"They are my blood," he said quietly, a slow smile breaking on his face. "They are my blood, my family, my children. They will live here. They will grow up here. They will learn Arabic, learn the ways of this great kingdom, the history of their family. They are mine, Pen. And so are you."

## 27

"A 6.25 percent match with my DNA," said the Sheikh as Pen listened even though she felt faint in the head and unsteady on her feet. "That means the children were born to a half-sibling of mine, someone who shares twenty-five percent of my DNA. The genetic math works out perfectly. They are my blood, and I am now their father."

"You're not their father," Pen said instinctively even as she felt her heart leap with a mixture of so many emotions that she realized she needed to sit down.

"Is he our daddy?" said one of the twins, looking up at her with a wide-eyed smile.

"Daddy," said the other, gazing directly at the Sheikh as if she'd already decided on the answer.

"Can we just . . ." Pen stammered, for once not sure what she was thinking, what she wanted to do, what she needed to say. "Can we . . ."

The Sheikh raised his arm and two veiled female attendants stepped forward from where they'd been standing like they were part of the purple velvet curtains in the background. The attendants had been with the kids day and night over the past few days, and the twins eagerly went with them, tugging their black gowns and drawing giggles from the mostly silent women.

Then the room was quiet, nothing but the gentle swish of warm air coming in through the large open balcony, the faraway sounds of the capital city in the distance, the in-and-out of her own breathing seemingly the loudest thing in her senses. Pen blinked as she carefully sat down on an overstuffed chair with a strong teakwood frame. The Sheikh was across from her on a matching divan, his legs up on the teakwood table upon which were a sheaf of papers.

*They are mine, and so are you.*

Pen looked Rafeez in the eye as she thought back to his words. In a way she'd known it would come to this. She'd known it from the way they'd laughed and joked together, from the way she trusted him to the core even when he'd acted like a goddamn psycho. She'd known it in the way he kissed her, the way he held her, the way he damned well took her like she was his and his alone. Hell yeah, she was his. And now they were bound by blood and genetics too: the blood of these kids.

Oh, God, Willow, you beautiful bitch, Pen thought as she felt a smile break on her face. You gave me everything before you died, didn't you? So why am I so fucking scared? Why am I still hesitant? Why?

Because you're not sure you deserve it, came the answer on the desert breeze. You're still wondering if it's a dream, a fairy-tale, an illusion. You knew that you were too good for a loser like David, but you're not sure if you're good enough for a man like Rafeez. And now that the kids turned out to be his sister's, you might never know if he truly wanted you or if he's just taking you as a part of a package deal, an obligation to take the mother along with the children.

That desert breeze picked up a bit just as the doubts began to play havoc with Pen's frazzled state of mind, and through her blurred vision she saw those papers rustling in the wind. She stared and blinked, frowning as she looked up into the Sheikh's green eyes.

"Are those the results?" she said, her frown cutting deeper as she saw the Sheikh's tight half-smile, caught the faraway look in his eye, noticed the way his fists were clenched like he was being racked by conflicting emotions as well: vulnerability and doubt mixed with a feeling of delight, joy, and excitement. "May I?"

The Sheikh grunted, uncrossing his legs and placing one big bare foot on top of the papers. Pen saw the color rush to his face, and she leaned over and firmly tugged at the sheaf of papers.

"Gimme it," she said, feeling that current of playfulness that had run through all the interactions with the Sheikh, no matter how serious. But Rafeez shook his head and placed another bare foot on the papers, and so Pen just shrugged, grabbed his ankle, and began to tickle the soles of those big brown feet.

The Sheikh roared with laughter, kicking out at her instinctively. The movement was just enough for Pen to slide the papers out from under his feet, and she screamed in triumph, holding them up as the Sheikh leaned forward and tried to swipe them from her hand.

She looked at the papers and squinted. Then she glanced at the Sheikh, noticing how the color had rushed to his face again, his green eyes narrowing, fists clenching like he was suddenly nervous, scared, vulnerable even though he was still smiling.

"I don't understand," she said softly, her voice catching in her throat as she stared at the results.

"That is because advanced genetics is probably beyond the comprehension of an American farmgirl," said Rafeez, taking advantage of her shock and snatching the papers from her hand.

"Oh, and an Arabian ape with gigantic, hairy feet understands it all, I suppose. What the hell, Rafeez? What's going on?"

The Sheikh swung his gigantic, hairy feet off the teakwood table and stood. He held the papers out in front of him, his green eyes narrowed and focused. "Here is what's going on. Here is the interpretation of these results. Here is your answer."

Then he ripped the papers to shreds, letting the white scraps fall to the red carpet like snowflakes in a North Dakota storm.

Pen stared as a feeling of surrealness washed over her, like she was imagining it all, imagining this Palace, imagining *him*. But she knew it was real, and she knew what he was saying, what he meant: He was saying the results meant nothing. He'd already decided that these were his children, that she was his woman, that they were going to be a family. It didn't matter if he was obligated to care for those children by the bonds of blood. He was saying he was choosing to care for them because of the bonds of love.

Love for her.

"Are you saying what I think you're saying?" Pen whispered, blinking as she watched the white pieces of paper drift to the carpet, swirl in the breeze, scatter across the room like confetti.

"What do you think I am saying?" Rafeez said, smiling as he took a step toward her.

"You say it first."

"I have already said what I need to say. The rest is in the doing."

"That doesn't even make sense," giggled Pen, blinking as she saw the front of the Sheikh's silk pajamas begin to rise. "And no, this isn't happening. My children are in the next room!"

"The walls are thick, my queen," the Sheikh grunted, pulling on the drawstring of his pajamas. "They will not hear you scream."

"You're sick!" Pen said, gasping as the Sheikh dropped his pajamas to reveal his cock filled out and hard, its upward curve beckoning to her like a finger saying "Come hither, woman."

"You know what they say about men with gigantic, hairy feet," the Sheikh grunted, stroking himself shamelessly as he strode up to her and placed his hands on her sides. He caressed her hips, pulled her gown up over her head, pinched her breasts hard through her bra until she squealed with pleasure.

"What about your vow to never have children?" Pen whispered as she watched him pull her bra off and then moaned as he shoved his mighty paws down the back of her panties, grabbing her ass with such force she almost choked.

"Well, I said I would give up the throne when I turn fifty-right, so we have a couple of decades to figure it out," Rafeez grunted as he pulled down her underwear in one swift motion. "Perhaps we will keep all our children a secret. Give them fake names, make them wear disguises in public, deny their existence when questioned by the media. Perhaps we will cut them out of my will, banish them to exile if they show any ambition to sit upon the throne." He paused, going down on his knees and steadying her so she could step out of her rolled-up panties. Then he turned her around and kissed her rear, reaching around to her front and rubbing her mound roughly as she leaned back into him. "Or perhaps I will only take you in the arse for the next twenty years."

Pen shrieked in mock horror as she felt Rafeez spread her rear globes and tease her hole with his tongue. "You're sick!" she said as she felt the wetness flow through her matted pubic curls and into the Sheikh's thick fingers. "And I'm sick for allowing you to have your way with me."

"Let us make one thing clear," the Sheikh said, standing up and pressing the head of his cock to her rear. "This is my kingdom, my Palace, and you are my queen. There is no question of permission or being *allowed* to have my way with you."

He pushed into her just as he said the words, and Pen's eyes rolled up in her head as she felt him slide in, nothing but his natural lubricant smoothing the way into her anus. At the same time he pushed three fingers into her pussy and curled them up against the front wall of her vagina, bringing forth an orgasm that was so sudden and explosive that Pen felt her own wetness shoot out all over the Sheikh's hand.

"Oh, God, what are you doing to me?!" she groaned

as she felt him drive into both her holes at once. She was powerless in his grasp, and she almost choked as Rafeez brought his free hand up along her body, pinching her breasts, rubbing her throat, and finally shoving his middle finger into her mouth as he pumped harder into her ass.

Pen sucked on his finger with everything she had, the sensation of being filled in all three holes so overwhelming she wasn't sure if she was crying or laughing. It was all the same suddenly, joy and sadness, fear and madness, life and death even . . . that place where all emotions were raw and nameless, where physical pleasure and spiritual ecstasy were indistinguishable.

She came again as she felt him explode in her ass, and for a moment she thought she was flowing from everywhere: Her saliva from the way she was sucking his finger, the wetness his fingers were bringing forth from her vagina, and the overflow from her rear as the Sheikh emptied his massive balls into her with frenzied, manic jerks that made every ounce of her flesh shiver and shake.

When he was done he pulled out of her, sliding his wet hands around her naked waist and dragging her over to an oversized day-bed that faced the open balcony. He tossed her down onto the soft mattress like she was a rag-doll, draping himself over her and kissing her bare shoulders and back as she shuddered from the aftermath of what he'd just done to her.

"Twenty years of that?" she murmured. "Oh, the burdens of being queen!"

"Actually it will be a lifetime of that," grunted the Sheikh. "But yes, just twenty or so years of being queen."

"What if I don't want to give up my crown in twenty years?" Pen whispered, giggling as she felt the Sheikh press up against her. "What if I hatch a conspiracy with my children to assassinate you when you're fifty-seven and seize power one year before Zahaar becomes a democracy?"

"Well, perhaps I will imprison you and all our children when I turn fifty-six, just to make sure nothing interrupts my noble plans."

"So then you'll visit me in the dungeons every night?" Pen whispered. "Feed me bread and water through the metal bars? Sounds romantic."

"Oh, it will be romantic, I assure you," the Sheikh said, laughing. "Especially when I spank your fifty-year old bottom for daring to oppose me."

"I doubt your gorilla-sized cock will still get hard at the sight of my wrinkled old butt in twenty years," Pen said, smiling and closing her eyes as she basked in images of the two of them spending a lifetime together.

"I will Botox your arse so it is smooth like a French teenager's," grunted the Sheikh, reaching between them and rubbing her rear.

Pen shrieked out loud. "OK, thanks for ruining the moment, you sick asshole!"

The Sheikh laughed, and Pen pushed back against him as she fought back tears of happiness. A part of her still felt some guilt that she was the cause of him going back on his vow to never have children. But then she realized that he wasn't going back on his word. He was making a compromise. He was issuing a challenge. He was saying that they'd have to find a way through this together, as a married couple, as man and woman, husband and wife . . . and most importantly as *parents*! How would they raise their children—both adopted and natural—to share the same values they'd chosen, to take a broader view of their responsibilities, their privileges, their gifts?

Pen felt a shiver go through her when she realized the road wasn't going to be easy. There'd be moments of doubt for them both. Hell, there was probably doubt in his mind right now! But he'd made a choice the moment he'd decided that the results of those DNA tests were irrelevant, that his heart was going to choose, that his heart had already chosen. Chosen her. Penelope Peterson. Her, and whatever came with her.

"All right," Pen said finally. "We should probably get back to the kids, yeah?"

"Yes," said the Sheikh without a moment's hesitation. "Let them know that I am Daddy, Father, and God-King to them from this moment forth."

Pen raised an eyebrow and also her left hand, sticking out her ring finger. "Um, not yet, Ape-man. Maybe in the animal kingdom you claim your mate with your cock. But in the human world you need to put a ring on it."

"We shall see," said Rafeez, slowly untangling himself from her and standing up.

"Excuse me? What the hell does that mean?"

"It means what it means."

Pen blinked as she wondered if the Sheikh was already having doubts about what he'd said. Then she wondered if it was her own insecurities that were making her think that he had doubts. And finally she shook her head and took a deep breath and reminded herself to calm the hell down and have some faith. Faith in herself. Faith in him. And faith in Willow, who'd put them together.

Then suddenly reality butted in and Pen glanced up at the Sheikh, tall, brown and naked in the sun. She thought of Willow, killed in a car crash. She pictured Randy, drowned in a bathtub. She saw an image of Charlotte Goodwin, calmly asking that Pen hand over the twins to her. This wasn't over. Hell no, it wasn't over.

## 28

"Stay over there," the Sheikh commanded, stopping in the doorway and holding his arm up so Pen wouldn't enter. "I said stay!"

"I'm not a dog!" Pen answered hotly, but she obeyed him, stopping a few feet behind the Sheikh. "What's going on? Are the children OK?"

"They are fine," the Sheikh said, hesitating as he surveyed the room. He could feel the dread rise up in him, but he knew he had to stay calm. If whoever did this had wanted to harm the twins, the children would already be dead. In fact they would have been dead in the car crash that killed Willow, or drowned in the bathtub along with Randy. The children were not in danger. But perhaps everyone else was.

The Sheikh closed his eyes and muttered a silent

prayer as he took in the sight of his two attendants sprawled on the carpet. The walls were indeed thick—so thick that neither Rafeez nor Pen had heard a thing. Not that they were paying attention, Rafeez thought. But regardless, the Sheikh decided as he glanced at the open balcony and then at the blood that was obscured by the red carpet: The gunshots would not have been heard. These were shots taken from far away. One shot for each target.

"What the hell?!" Pen screamed, and she pushed past the Sheikh and ran to the twins, pulling them both into her bosom and holding them close. They hugged her back, but they both seemed strangely calm, the Sheikh thought. Yes, they would not have heard the gunshots, and given that the attendants were probably just standing silently in the background watching the kids play, the children might barely have noticed anything was wrong at first. Still, it seemed unusual to say the least.

"Stay calm," the Sheikh said, frowning as his mind raced. Clearly this was a message. Someone was saying they could get to these children—and to whoever was protecting the children—at any time, in any place. Perhaps that was the message with Willow's death. The same with Randy. And now that it was the two of them as the sole guardians . . .

Suddenly Rafeez's eyes went wide as he glanced toward the open balcony. Ya Allah, what was he thinking! How could he be so stupid?!

"Get down!" he roared, leaping at Pen and the twins,

shoving them out of the way as a silent bullet thudded its way into the carpet. It took a moment for him to hear the distant sound of the gunshot, which told him the sniper was far away, perhaps on the rooftop of one of the high-rise hotels in the city center.

"What the fuck?!" Pen screamed, pulling the twins towards the door as she crawled along with them. "This can't be happening!"

"It is happening. But we are not in the line of fire now," said Rafeez, crouching down in front of Pen and the twins. In front of his family. "Still, we are not safe here."

"What do you mean we aren't safe here? This is a goddamn palace! There are walls, gates, and armed guards, right? How can we not be safe here?!"

"What I mean is it is not safe for anyone else here. Not as long as we are here." He glanced over at his slain attendants and then up at Pen, searching her panicked expression to see if she understood, if she would rise up, be strong for what he was going to suggest they do. "Pen, the children are not in danger. Whoever is doing this wants them alive, or else they would already be dead. It is the people around them who are in danger. I cannot put my people at risk like this." He took a breath and tightened his jaw. "I will take the children and leave the Palace in clear sight. Alone. I will draw them out, lead them to a place where I have the advantage. And then I will finish it."

Pen's eyes widened as her mouth opened like she wasn't sure what to say. Then she closed her eyes and shook her head. "You're insane. What the hell are you talking about? You're just going to get yourself killed, and I'll never see you or my kids again. No way. Absolutely not."

"So what do you suggest? We hide out in a saferoom with no windows, eating camel-jerky and sipping stale water for the rest of our lives while some unknown party wants us dead so they can steal our children?"

Pen snorted, her eyes wide with disbelief. "It's not an unknown party! It's that blonde witch Charlotte! It has to be! She's been after these kids from day one! So just send your people to her goddamn office in Fargo and have her brought here! Or better still, just have them put two bullets in her freakin' head for what she did to Willow and Randy! And your attendants!"

The Sheikh smiled as he saw the anger rise up in his woman, overcoming the panic he'd seen earlier. Good. She wasn't going to break. She wasn't going to cower down. His instincts about her were right. Ya Allah, what children they would have!

Rafeez pushed aside the thought that seemed to come out of nowhere. This was no time to be fantasizing about having children with her! Not when neither of them might make it out of the room alive!

"We do not know what role Charlotte has in all

this," the Sheikh said, blinking and focusing back on the matter at hand. He glanced over at the twins once again. They looked calm. Shockingly calm, like being around violence was nothing new to them, like it was in their blood, part of who they were. "She is a goddamn professor in North Dakota, Pen. Regardless of what she may or may not be capable of, she most certainly does not have the connections to engineer this kind of . . ."

He trailed off as he took one last look at his attendants lying dead on the hand-woven carpet. Once again he glanced over at the twins. They were the connection, he realized. They were the only ones who had the connection.

So what were the connections here?

Colombia?

Cartels?

Cocaine?

His mind travelled back to those days at Oxford when he'd first met Charlotte. She'd been a wild thing, partying every night like it was her last day on Earth. Alcohol, drugs, you name it. All of it flowed through the halls of Oxford after the sun went down, so it wasn't just her. But it had certainly been one of the reasons the Sheikh had never considered a serious relationship with her, and he did remember more than one occasion when he'd seen her measure out a line of white powder on his coffee table and snort it like she'd done it a hundred times.

## Grateful for the Sheikh

Rafeez thought back to his dead sister and her own addictions, her own drive to snort the white powder and revel in its high. It felt like there were connections here, but he couldn't make sense of it, couldn't get it straight in his mind. It could all be coincidence. After all, doing cocaine didn't mean you were directly involved with Colombian drug cartels!

But having your parents gunned down during a showdown between the Cartel and the Colombian Army might indeed mean you were involved, the Sheikh thought as he thought back to what Pen had told him about the twins' real parents and how they'd died. The official story was that it was accidental. A lot of accidental deaths seemed to be happening around these children.

Well, clearly things have escalated from being mere accidents, Rafeez decided as he ushered his chosen family out of the room after it had been several minutes without another bullet thudding into the walls or carpeting. We are past the point of elaborate fake accidents. This is real, and it is for keeps.

When they were out of the room and safely in the hallway, away from all windows and balconies, the Sheikh looked into Pen's eyes and nodded. "You have to trust me. We are not safe here. I will take the children alone, and I will end this. Trust me."

Pen snorted, rolling her eyes at him. "Right. You will take the children and leave me here. The moment you drive past the gates, I'll be slaughtered like a cow and buried in the desert somewhere. Then you'll have the kids, and Charlotte will join you, and the four of you will ride off into the sunset, laughing at what a moron I turned out to be."

The Sheikh rubbed his eyes and shook his head. "Ya Allah, Pen. This is not the time to talk like a crazy person! How can you believe this is some conspiracy between me and Charlotte?!"

"Because it is," came a cool, calm, controlled female voice from behind them. "It is a conspiracy between Rafeez and me. He just doesn't know it."

## 29

"Charlotte?" said the Sheikh, blinking as he stepped in front of Pen and the kids as if to shield them. "How did you get into the Palace?"

"Let's just say I know the password," replied the tall, blue-eyed woman as she leaned to her left and smiled at Pen. "Hello, Penelope! How was my half-eaten muffin?"

Pen clenched her fist and seriously thought about swinging it before she decided to give it a minute. She glanced at the Sheikh, and she could tell that his astonishment was genuine. So was his instinct to protect her and her children, and although Pen's head was swirling as she tried to figure out what the hell was happening, there was a strange sensation of warmth flowing through her as she felt the Sheikh's shadow fall across her and the kids like a blanket.

"The harlot's gate," muttered the Sheikh. "I told you about it as a joke when we were at Oxford." He turned sideways towards Pen. "A gate that was used in the old days when the Sheikhs would have women snuck into the palace after dark. It has a lock that is basically a puzzle, like a combination of moves." He glanced back at Charlotte. "You figured out the combination."

"I do have a PhD, you know," said Charlotte. She bent forward and looked at the twins. "Hello, you two! What are your names?"

"Don't answer her," Pen ordered.

"Don't worry. I already know their names," said Charlotte. She took a breath and smirked. "*All* their names. New and old. Yes, Carlos and Camilla? You remember the names your real parents gave you?" She pointed at the twins one by one. "You were named for your grandfather, Carlos Ramonas, head of the infamous Ramonas Family. And you, young lady, were named for your mother: Camilla Pedrera, princess of the Pedrera Family. Two of the most powerful families in the Colombian Drug Cartel."

Pen stared at Charlotte as her vision blurred for a moment before returning to focus. "You don't know that," she said weakly. "How could you know that when even the adoption agencies didn't know who their parents were?"

Charlotte laughed. "You really are an innocent farmgirl, aren't you? God, she's a real prize, Rafeez! This is the woman you chose over me?"

The Sheikh just stared at Charlotte. "Chose over *you*? Charlotte, I have not seen you in over a decade! There was never any question of choosing you over *anyone*, let alone Pen!"

Charlotte shrugged. "Fair enough. I've done better anyway. In twenty years you won't even be a king. And chances are, with oil prices going down, you won't even be a billionaire." She winked at Pen. "Gotta bet on the future, not the past, hon. Like Wayne Gretzky said, Skate to where the puck's going to be, not where it is now."

Pen snorted. "Is that a hockey reference? Wow, you really are a Midwestern gal, aren't ya."

"Part Canadian, actually. You know, that big country up north with thousands of miles of unpatrolled borders?"

"What in Allah's name are you talking about, Charlotte?" said Rafeez. "You are spouting nonsense. You are unhinged. Insane. Mad."

Charlotte sighed and shook her head. "Oh, yes. Just another hysterical woman spouting nonsense, says the Great Ape himself. Perhaps next you'll say I have my period."

"Everyone calls me an ape, and yet I am the one being accused of prejudice," grumbled the Sheikh. "All right. Go on, Professor. The floor is yours."

"Skate to where the puck's going to be, not where it is," Charlotte said triumphantly. "Oil is on its way out, but cocaine is coming back to America in a big way. The problem is, the route from Colombia has always been through Mexico, whose borders are being watched a lot more closely these days. But Canada . . . now that's a different story. The media doesn't give a damn about the Canadian borders, and so the politicians don't worry about spending money patrolling it. And North Dakota is right there. Yeah, it costs a bit more to fly the goods up to Canada, but we make up for it because so little gets seized at the border. Simple economics."

The Sheikh stared at Charlotte. "So this was all about . . . money?"

Charlotte stared right back. "Of course! It all starts and ends with money! Do you know how much a college professor makes? I have no intention of doing the lecture circuit when I'm sixty, you know. What, are you surprised?" She shook her head, glancing at Pen and smiling. "See, when someone is born into money they don't get it. You and I, we get it."

"Speak for yourself," Pen snapped. But then she turned red when she remembered she'd taken twenty million from the Sheikh in exchange for her turkeys.

Or was it twenty million in exchange for her values?

"Regardless," said the Sheikh firmly, and from his tone Pen could tell he had a plan in the works so she stayed with the children and let him lead. "You said this was a conspiracy between you and me. What did you mean?"

Charlotte took a breath and closed her eyes. "All right. I suppose you two deserve to hear the full story. So listen. The shootout that killed the twins' parents was just one of many in an ongoing escalation of the war between the Cartel and the Colombian Government—which of course was being supported by the American Drug Enforcement Agency. The Cartel could see that there was no way they could simply fight it out and hope to win—not with the Americans supplying the Colombian Army with weapons, intelligence, and training. So they decided to go dormant, to seed things for the next generation of the Cartel's top families. They sacrificed certain members of the family so others could get out of the country. Get out by way of adoption while covering up where they'd come from. The Cartel used the last bit of their influence to cover up birth records, to place the children of the Families all over the world, in Europe, America, Asia. Like sleeper agents, in a way." She paused and took a breath. "My husband was one of those children, sent to Canada for adoption. We met in Amsterdam a few years ago, and he told me that when he was eighteen, a member of the Cartel had contacted him and told him who he was. That was how it was planned for all of the children, spanning two or three generations. It's been going on for decades." She took another breath, narrowing her eyes with a strange satisfaction as she looked at the Sheikh. "And it started with your sister, Rafeez. She was one of the first sent away for adoption after the Cartel obscured her birth records. Except she returned to Colombia and got romantically involved with a member of the Ramonas family. Pure coincidence! Perhaps the pull of destiny! Anyway, they fell in love, eloped, and had children. Twins. A boy and a girl. Carlos and Camilla."

Pen saw the Sheikh's body reel as Charlotte spoke, and she could barely see straight when it hit her: A zero percent match on the DNA tests. But of course it would be zero percent if the Sheikh's sister had been adopted! So these *were* his sister's children?! Except she wasn't his real sister, she was adopted! Did he know?! Did he even know she'd been adopted?!

One look at the emotion on the Sheikh's face and Pen knew it was as much a surprise to him as it was to her. But this wasn't the time to be gasping at dramatic family revelations, because clearly Charlotte wasn't just telling them all of this to pass the time.

"Why are you telling us this?" Pen said, her voice almost a whisper. "What do you want?"

"You know what we want," Charlotte said softly,

*Grateful for the Sheikh*

glancing quickly at the twins and then back at Pen. "My husband and I want to be a family, to rebuild what was broken in generations past, to rebuild an empire based on providing pleasure in the form of a natural byproduct of the coca plant."

"Then you can start your own damned family," said the Sheikh, his voice confident and deep in a way that sent tremors through Pen. "Because this one is taken."

Charlotte glanced down and shook her head, and when she looked up again her blue eyes were cold steel "I told you what we want. So now I'll tell you what we *don't* want: We don't want anyone else to die. It's been a long, twisted path to get here, and we're not going to stop, but I'd rather not have anyone else die. This isn't about death. It's about life. See, my husband and I applied to adopt the twins ourselves, but we were denied because I failed a drug test. The test was confidential, so it didn't affect my job, but I was declared unfit to be a mother. Can you fucking believe that?! So anyway, my husband was about to pull the plug and just marry someone else, but I convinced him that by the time he got someone else on board with the whole thing, the twins might well be adopted by some other couple. Also, my husband wasn't an American citizen, so he needed the marriage to happen so he could stay in the United States. So we just kept track of the adoption process, and when the kids ended up with couple from Fargo—Willow and Randy—I took a job with the University of North Dakota. I figured once we were in the same city, we could maybe circumvent the adoption agencies and just go directly to the couple who got the twins!"

The Sheikh took a breath. "Ya Allah, Charlotte. Some things never change. People are just commodities that can be bought and sold, yes? Everything is up for negotiation, yes? You actually believed that convincing a couple to give up their adopted children was a reasonable plan of action?"

Charlotte shrugged. "That was only Plan A—which, I will admit, was far fetched." She glanced at Pen. "At first we offered cash to Willow and Randy, but they straight up said no. To be fair, we didn't have that much to offer, so perhaps that was it."

Pen rolled her eyes. "Yeah, I'm sure the amount was the only sticking point. I'm sure Willow would have sent the twins right over to you for the right number."

Charlotte blinked, but Pen didn't see any remorse in her blue eyes. "No. Willow wouldn't have. She was immovable, which was why we got her out of the way. But Randy . . . we had a chance there."

Pen gritted her teeth as she tried to hold herself back from just unleashing on this frigid, cold-hearted bitch. But she held back out of concern for those same children, Willow's children, her children now.

Charlotte went on, and Pen could see the glint in the woman's eye, like she was actually excited, thrilled even. *This woman thinks what she's doing is com-*

pletely justified, it occurred to Pen, and she shook her head and almost sighed as she listened.

"And I was close to an agreement with Randy. After Willow died—"

"You mean after you *killed* Willow," corrected Pen.

"Well, *I* didn't kill her," Charlotte said, almost shocked at the accusation. "My husband had it done. He's a quiet man, but very good at taking care of things."

The Sheikh turned his head slightly, not quite looking at Pen but in her general direction. Pen instinctively understood that she needed to hold her tongue here. For a little bit longer, at least. She needed to trust him.

"Go on," Rafeez said softly. "So you were close to an agreement with Randy. Then what?"

Charlotte shrugged. "Then my husband didn't want to wait any longer. He said it was pointless, that Randy was estranged from her parents, and if she died, they would be the next of kin. He figured it would be easier to get her parents to give up the kids, and so he had Randy taken out." She sighed and looked at Pen. "Of course, we missed the tidbit that little Miss Farmgirl was the godmother, next in line for the kids."

Pen nodded. "And so then you got to work on me. Though *you're* the piece of work in all this. How could you even *think* that any of us would give up our children?!"

"Hey, I wanted to be civil and reasonable about it!"

Charlotte barked, her white face going red alarmingly fast. "If my husband had his way, he'd have had everyone killed in fake accidents and staged suicides. If Willow hadn't been a stubborn little bitch, she'd still be alive. If Randy hadn't taken so damned long, she'd still be alive too. And if you had just signed over those little Colombian muppets, I wouldn't need to be here!"

"Why are you here, anyway?" the Sheikh casually asked, taking a step to his left, toward the door to the chambers where his attendants lay dead. "And you still haven't answered my question of how I'm involved in all this, about what you meant when you said we were in a conspiracy together—one which I'm not aware of, being the Great Dumb Ape of the East."

"You're her backup plan. A set-up for her Plan B," Pen said quietly as a chill rose up her spine. "In case Plan A failed, she knew she'd have to kill me too. And that would be too much of a coincidence. It wouldn't even be worth it to fake an accident, because no one would believe that three accidents could occur back-to-back, just coincidentally killing every person who happened to take custody of these children. So you were going to be the fall guy, Rafeez. The patsy. The turkey. She invited you for that wedding to bring you into the picture, place you in North Dakota, connect you to the scene." Pen paused and shook her head. "Was that even a real wedding, or was it just to have an excuse to bring Rafeez into town?"

Charlotte narrowed her eyes and smiled. "Very good, Farmgirl. The wedding was real enough, but you're right. We've been married for three years. The reception was just for Rafeez. To bring him into town. To establish the fact that he was there, in Fargo, just in case I needed to move to Plan B."

"Well, we're at Plan B. So now what?" Pen said.

"No more accidents. But I'll give you one last chance to come to an agreement with me," Charlotte said softly, and when Pen blinked and opened her eyes again the blonde Professor was holding a gun. "Or else I'll finish it here, and they'll never find your bodies. When the news leaks that the kids were Sheikh Rafeez's dead sister's offspring—the same Sheikh who was coincidentally in Fargo, North Dakota, not so long ago—it'll seem like he killed Pen, maybe even Willow and Randy, took the kids, and disappeared into the desert mist. A nice unsolved mystery that's outside the jurisdiction and reach of the Fargo police."

"You're insane," Pen said, snorting as she tried not to look at the gun. "This is a palace full of attendants and guards. Good luck dragging my fat dead ass through the hallways without anyone noticing! Not to mention you'll have two screaming kids in tow. And I'm sure once the first gunshot goes off, no one is gonna come to see who the hell is shooting at their Sheikh. Yup. Great plan, genius."

Charlotte seemed unperturbed. She glanced at the

kids and shrugged. "These kids aren't screaming. They're cool as ice, just like my husband. It's in their blood, Pen. They have a sense of their destiny, their birthright, where they came from, and they'll follow whatever path leads them back to it. You don't know what you're getting into here. You're not cut out for this. And no, I don't expect to shoot both of you and walk out of here. But I'll do it if you don't do what I say."

"Which is what?" said Pen.

"Accept a reasonable agreement. Just sign the adoption papers. It's so easy. It's the right thing to do." She looked at the Sheikh. "Rafeez, you swore you wouldn't have kids, and here you are turning your back on that vow for a woman! And you know what, that's great! Whatever floats your boat! So take your woman, and stick to your vow! Talk some sense into her! Don't make me do this! My husband was so close to just sending Cartel people in to finish this himself, but I told him to give me a chance to talk some sense into you."

Pen frowned at that last statement as she thought about the dead attendants in the next room. It seemed odd that Charlotte would say that when clearly Cartel people were already being sent in. She glanced at the Sheikh, and she knew he'd picked up on that too.

And then Pen got it: Shit, Charlotte didn't know that her husband had already sent people in to finish things his way!

So why the hell did he let her come to the Palace on this crazy mission?

"Three years," Rafeez said slowly, his eyes narrowing but not in anger.

"What?" said Charlotte.

"That is how long you have been officially married to your Canadian-Colombian husband, yes?"

Charlotte shrugged. "Yeah. So?"

"So three years is the official probationary waiting period before a green-card obtained through marriage becomes permanent. He is now an American and a Canadian citizen. Free to go anywhere in the world, pass across borders without much more than a wave of his passport. Your husband no longer needs you, Charlotte. You've done your job. Provided all the connections to the kids. Set me up as the fall guy who kidnaps the children and disappears into the desert. And then he sends you into the lion's den on a suicide mission. You've outlived your usefulness, Charlotte. I'm sorry."

Charlotte frowned as she looked down at the gun in her hand. Then she whipped her head around as if she was expecting to see armed guards swarming in on her. But there was no movement. The hallways were empty.

"You're not making any sense," Charlotte said. "The gun is just to show you I'm serious, or in case things got out of hand. I'm only here to talk, and my husband agreed that I should give you guys one last chance to work out an agreement. I'm just here to talk, you guys!"

"Well, your husband is clearly a man of few words," said the Sheikh, taking another step towards the open room, standing just out of sight of the balcony as he gestured with his head. "Take a look. Clearly he has proceeded with Plan B. Or is it Plan C now? C for Charlotte?"

Charlotte's frown cut deeper as she glanced into the room, and when Pen saw how the woman's eyes went wide at the sight of two dead bodies sprawled on the red carpet, she almost felt sorry for Doctor Charlotte Goodwin.

Almost.

The dull thud of the bullet hitting her body came a full second before the sound arrived, and Pen watched as if in a daze as the spatter of blood marked the yellow sandstone walls of the hallway. Charlotte went down silently in the doorway, her blue eyes still wide, the gun still in her hand.

"Oh, God," Pen gasped, closing her eyes and then turning to the kids. Once again they seemed relatively unaffected, and Pen thought back to what Charlotte had said about where these kids came from, what they'd seen as infants.

"Ya Allah," the Sheikh muttered, closing his own eyes for a moment as he took a long breath. Pen could tell he was affected by it, but she also knew he'd done what he needed to do by drawing her into the line of fire.

"How did you know?" Pen asked after a long moment of silence as the four of them stood safely out of view of the balcony. "I mean, how did you know her husband would take her out as well?"

"I knew it the moment Charlotte said it was about the money. It is never about the money. The money is just incidental." He shook his head and sighed. "The families of the South American Cartels—just like the families of the European Mafias—function like royalty of old. The goal is conquest, expanding the empire, exercising power and influence. Everything else is secondary. Everyone who is not of their blood is just a means to an end. Charlotte thought she knew what she was getting into, but she did not. And she paid the price." The Sheikh blinked, turning his head away from Charlotte's dead body. Suddenly his green eyes were narrowed with focus, alert with urgency. "And so will we if we do not hurry. Come. It is time to take this battle out to the desert. To my hunting grounds. To where I have the advantage. Come, my queen. Come."

## 30

Pen stared at the swaying desert palms rising up like a mirage, the tall trees looming over the thick foliage of a miscellany of desert plants. It looked like a tropical island had been transposed to the middle of the barren desert, and she had to rub her eyes to make sure she wasn't seeing things.

"That's the Great Oasis?" she said softly as the Sheikh maneuvered the Range Rover over the last of the dunes and onto the flat sand leading to the edge of the Oasis. "Looks more like the Great Jungle!"

"It is a myth that the desert is a barren wasteland," said the Sheikh. "The Great Oasis supports almost four hundred acres of greenery and wildlife. I know

Grateful for the Sheikh 231

it like the back of my hand. Once we are in here, it eliminates any chance of a sniper catching sight of us. They will have to follow us in here. Engage us at close quarters. And we will see them coming long before they see us, I guarantee."

Pen glanced in the rearview mirror at the twins. They were strapped securely in the backseat, both of them earnestly staring out of opposite windows like this was a trip to the zoo. Then she glanced down by her feet and shook her head when she saw the wooden box full of bullets for the Sheikh's hunting rifle, which was secured in the trunk.

"I still don't understand why we aren't taking an army of guards out here with us," Pen said, even though at the heart of it she did understand. She understood the Sheikh's primal need to finish things himself, on his own terms, on his own damned turf. "Charlotte's husband might send an army of Colombian mercenaries with grenade-launchers and machine-guns in there!"

The Sheikh smiled calmly, and Pen could tell there was a part of him that was excited by the looming showdown. God, he *is* an ape, an animal, an alpha beast! And I love him. Shit, I love him!

"Remember, the children are the priority," he said in that calm voice which somehow reassured Pen this was going to work even though this man had decided it was a better plan to drive his woman and kids out to the goddamn desert than to hide in his Palace and send out his armed guards to do their jobs and protect their king! "He cannot risk the children being harmed, and so he will not send in a bunch of trigger-happy thugs. We will have the advantage here, Pen. Trust me."

Pen closed her eyes and took a breath as the Sheikh barreled the Range Rover past the edge of the foliage. Suddenly the sun seemed like it was blocked out, and a cool shade descended on the car. The Sheikh drove as far as he could, but the undergrowth soon got so thick he had to stop.

"We go on foot from here," he said softly, turning and smiling at the kids. "You two ready for a hike with Daddy and Mommy?"

The twins nodded in unison, and Pen just stared at them and shook her head. Their resilience amazed her, and in that moment she understood what Charlotte had said about what was in their blood, their makeup. She also understood what the Sheikh had said about these families being a throwback to the Royals of old. These kids certainly seemed poised as if they could handle anything. Shit, they'd make a great king and queen, wouldn't they?

"Shouldn't they stay in the car?" Pen asked as she hesitantly stepped out of the bulletproof Range Rover and looked down at the desert shrubs that rose almost to her knees.

*Grateful for the Sheikh*

"They stay with us. The closer they are to us, the closer our enemies have to come," said the Sheikh.

Pen stared at him. "Am I hearing you right? Are you saying that our kids are bait?"

Rafeez shrugged, smiling at her, that glint in his green eyes telling her that he was in a zone, the zone of an animal, a fighter, a protector. Someone who would do what it took to win. "Yes. And since Charlotte's husband cannot risk hurting them, they will have to get close to get to us, and I will see them coming. Pick them off one by one."

The Sheikh patted his hunting rifle, which Pen had watched him clean and load before they'd left the safety of the car. This all still seemed insane, but in a way it also made complete sense. Either way, they were here, all four of them, a weird-ass family trudging through knee-high desert shrubs on their way to a violent showdown with the Colombian Cartel. Just another family vacation. Nothing to see here. Move along, please!

"Here," said the Sheikh, stopping at a dense cluster of cacti with thick, rounded stems that looked like they could stop a bullet. "We make our stand here."

# 31

"**S**tand still and do not move," commanded the Sheikh, glancing at the two kids and smiling at them. "We are right behind you. Nothing will happen to you. I promise."

"This is insane," said Pen. "No way. I can't allow this, Rafeez. This is just wrong."

"It is the only way. We need them to see the children so they know they cannot come in with guns blazing."

"*They*? I thought you said it was just gonna be the husband!" Pen whispered furiously.

"I said it wouldn't be an army of mercenaries, but it will not be just one man either," replied the Sheikh as he positioned his rifle between the cactus stems and adjusted the sight. "Three, maybe four men in total. Especially since they would have seen us driving out of the Palace without an armed escort. If we had stayed in the Palace, the chances of them bringing more men to storm the gates or scale the walls would be much greater. And although I have an armed Palace Guard, none of them have ever been in combat. We are a kingdom of peace, Pen. My so-called armed guards spend their days standing at attention and posing for photographs!"

"Oh, and *you're* ready to kill four trained assassins?" Pen said.

"It is a bit late for this discussion, don't you think?" said the Sheikh, turning to her sternly though he wanted to smile at his farmgirl. "We are here now. And there is only one way out."

"Yes," said Pen. "That way. Back to our bulletproof car. Back to our fortress of a Palace, where we wake up your guards and tell them to do their freakin' jobs!"

"Protecting his family is a man's job, and he must do it himself," said Rafeez. "Now if you will not help, then at least shut up so I can concentrate."

Pen started to say something, but the Sheikh held up his hand to stop her.

"What is it?" Pen said, cocking her head as the Sheikh squinted and slowly released the safety on his automatic rifle. "That doesn't sound like just three or four men, Rafeez! It sounds like a goddamn army!"

The Sheikh squeezed the trigger just as Pen spoke, and the rifle sounded like thunder. The children both jumped and turned, but the Sheikh could tell they were not frightened. Perhaps it was because they trusted him to protect them. Perhaps it was because they had been around gunfire and explosions when they were so young that it seemed normal now. Either way, he knew he could rely on them to stay still.

He fired again, taking down another shadowy figure moving through the thick foliage surrounding the Great Oasis. But a chill rose up in him when he realized Pen was right. This wasn't just three or four men. It seemed like a goddamn army—at least twenty that he could count, perhaps more, judging by the sounds of the dry shrubs and desert-grass being trampled underfoot as they closed in.

"Ya Allah," he muttered under his breath, taking aim and bringing down another foot soldier. "What is his plan here? Does he no longer give a damn about the children?"

He fired again, and then the Sheikh realized that although he'd killed three or four of them, he hadn't heard a single shot being fired in response! He'd underestimated the resolve of this man, and of the Cartel's foot-soldiers. He squinted as some of the men finally came into view, and immediately his chilling suspicion was confirmed: None of them were carrying guns.

## Grateful for the Sheikh

"What's going on?" Pen whispered. She'd been standing by his side, holding her ground even though the Sheikh could tell that every ounce of her wanted to rush to those children and shield them with her body. But she was smart and willful enough to follow the Sheikh's orders, trust his judgment that no harm would come to the children, that no one in the Cartel would risk even putting a scratch on their precious skin, draw even a drop of their protected blood. "Why aren't they shooting back? Are they worried about hitting the kids, just like you said?"

Rafeez shook his head grimly as he hit another man in the shoulder, sending him whirling away as blood sprayed up like mist. "They do not have guns. Just hunting knives. This is a suicide mission, Pen. They have sent too many for me to gun down. They will get to us sooner or later, no matter how many I kill. Ya Allah, it is a goddamn suicide mission! We need to retreat."

But the moment he said the words he heard the stomping of combat boots from all sides, and he knew they were surrounded. It was over. He and Pen would be gutted like fish, and the children would be claimed by Charlotte's husband. The man had played along with Charlotte's convoluted strategy of adopting the children for three years—long enough for him to become a United States citizen so he could freely travel through most of the world, back and forth across the Canadian border with ease. Then he'd eliminated Charlotte and gone directly after what he wanted. In a way Rafeez almost respected him. The man's blood ran cold, but it also ran royal. He cared for his bloodline and nothing else. Everything else was just a means to an end. So simple. So primal.

A feeling of strange gratitude came over the Sheikh as he lowered his weapon and prepared to engage the enemy at close quarters. He had a hunting knife of his own, and he could take any one of these men in single combat without breaking a sweat. Two, three, five . . . maybe seven. But not many more. Not if they swarmed.

The Sheikh glanced at the children, who for the first time were showing some fear as the foot soldiers drew close enough for everyone to hear their grunts, see their grimaces, smell their sweat.

The children will be OK, he thought. It is my woman who must be protected until the end. Until my last breath. Until my hand drops the knife. And that will only happen when I am dead.

"Stand behind me," said the Sheikh, reaching out and pulling Pen close as he drew his hunting knife and clenched his teeth. "No matter what, do not leave my side, do you understand?"

He saw her nod, her pretty round face almost drained of blood. But she didn't cry. She didn't run. She stood by him like his queen, and in that moment the Sheikh knew she would die by his side if it came to that.

Rafeez almost burst into tears as he felt a sudden warmth fill his heart, a deep sense of love, connection, and most of all gratitude. Gratitude. He was grateful, more than anything else in that moment.

"If this is the end, my American farmgirl," he said, turning and looking her in the eyes, knowing instinctively that she was feeling the same overwhelming sense of gratitude for the depth of emotion they'd shared in their time together. "Then it was worth it. I am grateful for every moment we spent together. Every damned moment, you understand?"

She nodded, her red lips trembling. "I know," she whispered. "Me too. Every moment, Rafeez. I'm grateful too. Grateful for everything. Thank you for coming into my life. Thank you for being there until the end."

She burst into tears at the same time he did, and when they kissed it was like everything around them disappeared and it was just the two of them again, the two of them in a North Dakota snowstorm, Thanksgiving around the corner, gratitude in the air.

The Sheikh held the kiss as long as he dared, but then suddenly Pen pulled away, cocking her head as she blinked and stared into the distance.

"What the hell . . ." she muttered, her eyes going wide as an incredulous smile began to break on her face. "Is that . . . no fucking way. It is! Ohmygod, it is!"

The Sheikh opened his mouth to ask what the hell Pen was talking about, but when he turned he saw it. He saw them.

All two hundred of them.

Beaks open wide.

Eyes bugged out and wild.

Two hundred turkeys, pissed off as hell, coming in hot, coming in hard, coming for Mama.

## 32
## __THREE WEEKS LATER__

"**O**hmygod, I can't get over how those guys ran!" Pen said, covering her eyes as she shook her head in disbelief at the memory, wondering like she'd done a hundred times whether that had actually happen. "Rafeez, did you see those guys run? They were screaming louder than the freakin' turkeys! Holy shit, I've never seen anything like it!"

The Sheikh had to put down his steaming teacup before his own laughter made him spill it all, and even the kids joined in, the twins running around the sprawling day-chambers of the Royal Palace's Eastern Wing, flapping their arms like turkeys as they gobbled and cackled and tried to reproduce the cacophony of noises produced by two hundred turkeys charging with everything they had.

The makeshift family of four laughed as long as they could. They laughed because it was the only thing they could do. There was no other way to deal with what had happened. There was no other way to thank whatever powers had sent those birds to the rescue. Laughter and gratitude: That was the only way.

Finally the sun was gone and the twins were ushered off to bed, leaving the Sheikh and his bride-to-be alone.

"So the Royal Tailors took my measurements for the wedding gown this afternoon," Pen said. "I've never been so embarrassed. I think they had to use two measuring tapes to get around my ass."

"Wait until you are pregnant and you have to get fitted for an entire new wardrobe," the Sheikh said without flinching.

Pen frowned at him. The past three weeks had been stressful, with all kinds of authorities involved after Charlotte's husband was arrested trying to cross the border into Saudi Arabia. Although the Sheikh had initially wanted to prosecute him under Zahaari law for an attempted assassination—a charge that carried the penalty of death—he'd finally agreed to hand him over to the CIA, who wanted to "debrief" the husband

*Grateful for the Sheikh*

at Guantanamo Bay: a process guaranteed to last for the rest of the man's life.

It was just a week ago that the Sheikh had walked into the room and announced that a wedding date had been set, and although Pen's heart had jumped, she'd been a little disappointed at the lack of show. Sure, he'd sorta proposed to her earlier, and she'd sorta said yes. But then he'd sorta been wishy-washy about it, and when he'd just put it out there again like it was a done deal she'd almost been indignant. A part of her wanted the fairy-tale proposal. Not to mention the—

"I have your ring," the Sheikh suddenly said, breaking her out of the daydream that was making her a bit grumpy. "It took a while, because it required some finesse to manufacture. It also required courage to acquire the raw materials. I have several scratches and beak-shaped holes in my arm to show for it."

Pen frowned as she wondered what the hell the Sheikh was talking about, and then she squealed in surprise when he went down on one knee and pulled out a big blue box, its lid already open, a gigantic diamond staring up at her . . . a gigantic diamond mounted on the shining, polished, smooth claw-nail of a turkey.

"Oh, my God," Pen said, not sure whether to laugh or squeal again. "How on Earth did you—"

"Trust me, woman, no turkeys were harmed in this

operation. I cannot say that no human was harmed, though. It appears turkeys do not like having their toenails clipped." The Sheikh shrugged and winked at her, feigning annoyance as Pen squealed again. "So will you marry me, my American farmgirl?"

## 33
## ONE MONTH LATER
## THE WEDDING NIGHT

"This is the first time, my queen. The first time I will come inside you."

Pen giggled as she felt the Sheikh's strong hands find their way through her wedding skirts, his fingers firmly lodging in the waistband of her panties and ripping them down the seam. "Oh, no! I was gonna wear those panties again!"

"You are a queen now," growled the Sheikh as he rubbed her between her ample thighs, his touch bringing forth her wetness along with a moan. "You will never wear the same panties twice. In fact, you will never wear panties again. I command it!"

Pen gasped as the Sheikh stood at the foot of the wedding bed and undressed, ripping the buttons off his black silk *sherwani* jacket, pushing down his tailored trousers, rolling down his underwear. Soon he was naked, his bronzed body rippled with muscle, his cock looking monstrous under the elegant chandelier made of hand-cut crystal. She was spread wide on the bed, her wedding dress up over her breasts, her slit exposed and wet for her king, for her Sheikh, for her damned husband.

"I know you've joked about it a few times, Rafeez," she whispered as she watched him stroke himself and then get on the bed with her, kneeling between her thighs and rubbing her clit with his cockhead until she was dripping all over the clean white sheets. "But we never seriously talked about the pregnancy thing again. We have two children, and nothing's gonna change that. But I know you made a vow, and I want you to know that I'm willing to help you keep that vow. I'll be willing to help you keep it every day, every night, every week, every year. Just like I did our first night together. I promise you, Rafeez. I'll—"

"You'll do nothing every day, every night, and every week except take my cock inside you and milk it until my balls are dry," the Sheikh said with barely an inflection in his voice, calmly sliding his massive shaft all the way deep into her as he said it.

Pen screamed in shock, both at the sensation of being filled so completely without warning as well as from the explicit image the Sheikh had conjured up with his words. Every day, every night, every week . . . spreading for him, taking him in, milking him dry!

"Oh, shit," she moaned as Rafeez began to pump into her like he couldn't hold back, couldn't control himself, didn't want to control himself. "Oh, God, that feels so . . . so . . . oh, *God*, Rafeez!"

Within minutes the Sheikh had exploded into her, his seed flooding her valley with such force that it seemed to drown out her own orgasm. She screamed as he drew back and pumped into her again, and then she clenched her pussy and milked him just like he'd said, just like he'd commanded, just like he'd damned well ordered.

One last push and he was done, and Pen closed her eyes and smiled when she realized how badly he'd wanted to come inside her. She dug her fingers into his hair, her smile getting wider as she listened to him pant against her neck like an exhausted beast.

"As I was saying," Rafeez finally said when he caught his breath. "Every night you will take my seed. And every year you will bear me a child. Every year until I am fifty-eight."

"Excuse me? What?" Pen said, grabbing his hair and pulling his head away from her so she could look at him. "Are you insane?"

"Perhaps. But that is what I have decided. Since I

cannot live with the prospect of never having a child with you, I have decided to go to the other extreme. The end result will be the same."

"How in God's name is the end result gonna be the same? How is having no kids the same as having like . . ." Pen frowned as she tried to do the math. "Ohmygod, having like twenty or thirty kids!"

"The effect will be the same. I wanted no kids so no one would claim the throne after I decided to transition the kingdom to democracy. But if I have thirty or more children, then how in Allah's name will they ever get organized enough to mount any serious threat to my plan for a permanent transfer of power?"

Pen laughed and shook her head. "I thought we'd decided that the pressure would be on us as parents to raise our kids right, to channel their ambition into worthy pursuits instead of just empty power and a fancy throne."

The Sheikh nodded. "That is Plan A. This is the backup plan."

Pen closed one eye and twisted her mouth as she glanced at the Sheikh. "Me carrying thirty of your gigantic ape-babies is a backup plan? Easy for you to say, big shot!"

The Sheikh sighed, turning towards her until she could feel his cock hardening again. "There is always a third option, my curvy farmgirl queen. Plan C."

"What's Plan C?" Pen whispered as she felt the

Sheikh's hands slide between her rear cheeks, his fingers spreading them, his big thumb resting squarely on her just-married, officially royal, rear pucker.

"Plan C is that I could just take you in the arse every night for the next thirty years," said the Sheikh as he flipped her onto her stomach like she was a rag-doll, pushed her wedding dress up over her head, raised her royal rump and spanked it hard.

"Ohmygod, you're disgusting!" she squealed as he spanked her again, then lowered his face to her rear and licked her long and deep.

"Why? Is that not a good ending for our romance story, my queen?"

"A romance story with your gorilla-sized cock stretching me wide every night for thirty years? Sounds more like a damned horror novel," groaned Pen as she felt the Sheikh open her up from behind. "And romance readers don't like horror messing up their happy endings. Not now. Not ever."

But still always . . .
And still forever . . .

∞

Thanks for sticking with me through 16 novels.
Happy Thanksgiving to you all.
Gratitude and love,
Anna.

## From Annabelle Winters

Thanks for reading.

Join my private list at **annabellewinters.com/join** to get steamy epilogues, exclusive scenes with side characters, and a chance to join my advance review team.

And do write to me at **mail@annabellewinters.com** anytime. I really like hearing from you.

Love,
Anna.

Made in the USA
San Bernardino, CA
15 January 2020